Exchanging Pleasantries

screenplay format included

by
ferf ziamond

Bloomington, IN  Milton Keynes, UK

AuthorHouse™
1663 Liberty Drive, Suite 200
Bloomington, IN 47403
www.authorhouse.com
Phone: 1-800-839-8640

AuthorHouse™ UK Ltd.
500 Avebury Boulevard
Central Milton Keynes, MK9 2BE
www.authorhouse.co.uk
Phone: 08001974150

© 2006 ferf ziamond. All rights reserved.

No part of this book may be reproduced, stored in a retrieval system, or transmitted by any means without the written permission of the author.

First published by AuthorHouse 2/28/2006

ISBN: 1-4259-1641-4 (sc)

Printed in the United States of America
Bloomington, Indiana

This book is printed on acid-free paper.

for
everyone who cares for a
clean and peaceful world

Contents

Novel Format   1
Screenplay Format   101

CHAPTER ONE

A soft breeze brings slight movement to the orange leaves that barely cling to the maples up and down Carter Bend. The street named after Vince Carter, the man who built the streets of Beverly Massachusetts. His memory is held alive through a bronze statue that sits proudly guarding the cul-de-sac at the end of the road.

Carter Bend forks off of Trenis' De Beverly Drive, which is the main road that runs through the entire town of three by three and a half miles. Where they meet is where Trenis' Village begins, an area of three streets comprised of a barber shop, gas station, ice cream shop, grocery store, library, and the coffee shop that has the appearance of an old shack.

A few friendly faces pass on the street throughout the day. A hello is never heard without someone's name to follow. Everyone knows everyone, and where those two roads meet is where most of the younger folks meet. Unkempt, historic in appearance, and never empty, the coffee shack is commonly a gathering place for the twenty-two to twenty-nine year olds. That doesn't mean that it can't have a couple of seventy year olds occupying a table every now and again.

Harper and Grump are two regulars who use the same table day after day to drink coffee and play checkers for hours upon

ferf ziamond

hours. Their minds are set back to their childhood era. They are sometimes referred to by the younger generation as, *the ugly versions of the Vince Carter Statue*. That is due to their being permanent fixtures and not the easiest on the eyes.

Their table, like the others, is made from old wood. All of the furniture looks as if it would fall to pieces if a strong wind came along. It looked like that since the first time Harper and Grump drank coffee at the shack.

Grump shakes his head and blinks his eyes rapidly. He looks around the room noticing a few more customers that must have slipped in while he nodded off. "Whose turn is it anyway?" He blurts to Harper who is not paying any mind to the game either.

"Hell if I know. My mind got lost out the winda." The small window facing Ludlum Avenue, the third of the three village streets, has cob webs in the corners and crust scattered along the panes. Through the weeds growing on the opposite side of the glass, a young woman can be seen on her way to the coffee shack.

A once gold set of chimes, now brown, shakes and rings as the door opens. "Mornin Dangie." Harper lifts his head for a moment and then looks back down at the checker board shrugging his shoulders. "Am I red or black?"

"Hi ya Harper." Dangie, mid twenties, brunette, cute but not a super model, walks

Exchanging Pleasantries

in unfolding some singles that she pulls from her purse. "The usual Kamptin." She lays two dollars beside the old fashioned register and smiles at the large man in a tank top behind the counter. His hair is dark and messy as is his beard.

"Dangie." Kamptin acknowledges her and places her cup of coffee on the worn counter.

She picks it up and walks past Harper and Grump's table. "Who's winning?" She looks at the checkerboard and takes a seat two tables back.

"I think I am." Harper looks up as the chimes ring again. "Oh, this character."

A young man in his twenties walks toward the counter. Kamptin reaches over to shake his hand. They speak for a few seconds and then the man heads toward Dangie holding his cup. "Black winning?" He looks at Grump.

"Black's always losing in my book." Grump stares him down as he takes a seat across from Dangie.

"Hey Dangie." He looks at her with his glowing blue eyes.

"Mort. Good morning. Starting in already?"

"Candyland is friendlier!" He lifts himself up, peering at Grump. Dangie lets out a giggle and covers her mouth. Mort was referring to the game candyland and how it would sooth rather than rile. Grump and Harper's old fashioned beliefs are the cause of their prejudice.

3

ferf ziamond

Grump looks back at Mort for a moment before Harper interrupts. "Gladstone's on his way up the street. He can get us a refill." His attention is out the window again.

"Thank you young man, you're very enlightening." Grump turns his head back to Harper and whispers. "What the hell is candyland?"

The chimes ring again and Harper smiles. "Hey Gladstone, would you mind?" He holds his coffee cup up to let the young man know he needs a refill. Grump follows suit.

The young man, the same age as Mort and Dangie, looks over and smiles back. He has a bag over his shoulder with a logo on it. TRENIS' TIMES. "Sure thing Harper, Grump." His name is MC but for some reason Harper and Grump refer to him as Gladstone. He looks further back and sees his friends. "Hey Mort. I may have done it!" He holds up a piece of paper and then looks back at Kamptin who places three cups and a package of crackers on the counter. A splinter comes up from the wood.

Over at the table Mort puts on a face and ridicules MC. "He may have done it once again. I may just pay a newspaper to hire him at this point."

"Oh that's so mean. He tries so hard. And he's so adorable." Dangie has an obvious crush on MC.

"Yea, your brother." Mort looks toward MC who is balancing three coffee cups on

Exchanging Pleasantries

his way to Harper and Grumps table. He looks back at Dangie. His straight face becomes a sarcastic grin. "Maybe now we'll be able to get his cell phone number." He continues abusing his friend. "Better yet, now maybe he'll stop talking about that website he puts his stories on."

MC makes his way over stopping by Harper and Grump to drop off their coffees. Harper hands him a dollar. "Keep the change Gladstone." The total cost was close to two dollars. MC doesn't mind picking up the rest of the bill.

"Thanks Harper." He folds the bill and slips it into his shirt pocket and then sits next to Mort, across from Dangie. "I'm out of here guys."

"What do you mean?" Dangie is quite concerned.

"I got a call. It's time to move on."

"On your Boston Herald phone?" Mort cracks a smile and drinks his coffee. MC always carries a cell phone around with him. None of his friends are allowed to have the number. It's reserved only for call backs regarding his ten or eleven job applications to The Boston Herald.

MC is a part time writer of novellas and short stories. His big dream is to become a writer for a big newspaper or magazine. This is the day he decides to tell his friends that his dream has come true.

"Nah. This is the big time. New York Newsday."

ferf ziamond

"Are you serious?" Dangie appears to be nervous.

Mort tries to stay relaxed. "You're really gonna go down there? What's wrong with your Trenis' Times gig?"

"Give me a break. The biggest pay I ever got for writing for them was this bag." He holds the bag up.

"Them black kids'll eat you alive. You don't stand a chance." Grump puts in his two cents and turns back around.

They just laugh to themselves. "What is wrong with that idiot?" Mort shakes his head.

"You'd be a grump too if your daughter in-law ran off with your grandson." Dangie is still focused on MC as she tries to explain Grumps anger.

"Even worse, not ever meeting that daughter in-law or grandson." MC smirks.

"Better for the daughter in-law and grandson. They don't need to know this grouch of a granddad." Mort laughs slightly at his own joke then he recalls a moment. "I met the grandson once. It's no wonder Grump's son kept a lid on that whole part of his life. Grump never would have approved. I could never forget that kid."

"C'mon, he's just an old man. He doesn't realize half of what he says." MC doesn't get annoyed by Grump's comments. "Do you think I should worry about the black kids?" He grows concerned.

Exchanging Pleasantries

"I can't believe you're actually considering leaving us." Dangie wipes a tear from her eye. "What are you going to do with Ferf?" Ferf is MC's grayish, black Ocicat that he had for the last five years.

"He's coming with me."

"That's a long ride. That might not be good for her."

"He'll be fine."

"She wasn't so great last time she was in a car."

Mort interrupts their conversation. "Five years and neither of you know the sex of that damn cat." He shakes his head.

At the same time Dangie and MC state their beliefs. "She's a girl!"

"He's a boy!"

"Exactly!" Mort looks up at MC. "So, you're really gonna do this?"

"I don't have a choice."

"Remember what I said when you're laying on the ground somewhere looking up at some black kid begging for your life." Grump chimes in again.

MC didn't really get called by Newsday. He uses that as a cover for his regular job relocating him to the New York office. Mort and Dangie are well aware of his writing dream so he feels that the best way to get them to understand his move is to say it is to chase that dream.

CHAPTER TWO

Light rainfall glides against the tall buildings. The streets are filled with yellow taxis at red lights. Pedestrians with umbrellas are on every corner. The honking of car horns indicates that this is lower Manhattan.

Between two fifty story buildings and off to the side, a big gold and black store sign sticks out on a three story building. MARIGOLD CAFÉ.

The inside of the café is a tremendous step up compared to the coffee shack. The door alone is made from the finest materials. Walls and floors of marble, ceiling fans, chandeliers, each modernized table and chair set complete with its own internet connection. Off to the side is a large shelf of exotic cookies.

Patrons set up scattered offices sipping lattes, coolatas, Mocha chinos, cremalinas, frappaccinos, creamy dippen frattas and any other silly named cup worth nine dollars and seventy five cents per half a serving.

One customer stands out above the rest. A yuppie named Ned. Tall, thin, mid-thirties, short blonde hair with plenty of mousse, someone the waitress' are not crazy about. He takes up two tables. Laptop, fratte latte, and newspaper on one. Briefcase, cell phone, beeper, scattered folders, and pages of notes on the other.

Exchanging Pleasantries

He takes his eyes away from the laptop momentarily as a waitress carrying a coffee pot passes by. "Another Fratte latte Ginger." He holds up his cup.

She has a perturbed look about her. "Ginger hasn't worked here in months." She walks to the counter and whispers to another waitress. "He's such an asshole."

The other waitress, cute, quiet, and easy going, laughs and hands her a cup. "One fratte latte."

The angry waitress wears a name tag labeled ANN. She takes the cup. "Yea, I hope he chokes on it."

The cute one wears the same type of tag. Hers is labeled DABNI. "You're too much."

"His arrogance is too much." Ann brings the cup to him as a phone is heard ringing behind the counter. "You got that Dabni?"

Dabni picks up the phone. It's her dad. She is excited to hear from him and she speaks loudly. "Daddy I miss you! How are things at home?"

In a small town outside of Boston, her dad, early fifties, a short, well groomed, pleasant man sits in a cozy, brown and white, neatly furnished kitchen. Scattered pictures held by magnet ornaments fill the refrigerator door. Dabni can be seen in a couple of the photos. A sign on an ornamental chef reads, NO BITCHIN IN GINNY'S KITCHEN.

ferf ziamond

On a windowsill sits a small birdhouse with a fake parakeet sitting on a perch.

Her dad has an enormous smile. "Come on home baby. I can set you up with your own place if you're ready."

"You know I'd love that daddy, but this just isn't the time. Besides, when it is time, I'll be setting myself up."

"I know you will honey." Some rattling is overheard in the background. "Oh wait baby."

"Daddy?" She becomes concerned. "Is everything okay?"

"I have to go for now baby." He is distracted. "You're mother just spilled some coffee on herself. I have to clean her up."

"Is she all right?"

"I'll give you a call later."

"Dad?"

"She'll be fine sweetheart."

Ann looks to Dabni as she slowly puts the phone down. "Is everything all right?"

"It always comes down to coffee in my life."

CHAPTER THREE

In front of the coffee shack, Dangie and MC stand facing one another. Dangie's dungaree jacket is two sizes too big. MC's hooded sweat jacket is rather snug. The wind messes their hair slightly.

Dangie is looking for reasons for MC to stay in Beverly. "How are you going to break it to little Francis? He'll be crushed."

MC looks at her as if she lost her memory. "Oh c'mon. Little Francis? How long has it been? Little Francis is not little anymore and I haven't done Tag Along since he turned sixteen a few months ago."

Tag Along is a Big Brother type organization that MC belonged to for close to five years. He helped to mold and turn a boy named Francis into a responsible young adult.

"Yea, I guess."

"Why are you reaching for this stuff? It's not making my situation any easier."

"Having a brother like you don't make my life any easier either. I have a situation too you know."

"What situation is that?"

"I could have a situation."

"Can you get on with it? I'm tired of the word situation already." His eyebrows point inward. "And stop calling me your brother!"

"You might as well be."

ferf ziamond

"Why is that?" MC appears to be put out.

"What other reason could you have for not sleeping with me?"

"Oh don't do this to me again Dangie." On one hand her crush makes it dificult for him to pack up and leave. On the other hand getting away might just be what their relationship needs. "And how'd you get such a silly name anyway? Dangie?"

"You're the bozo that gave me that name. My name is Angie, not Dangie."

"Oh yea, that's right." MC begins to walk down the sidewalk. Dangie follows. "Look, it's not gonna be forever. And it's not even that far."

"Can I visit you there?"

"Let's not push it."

"I always wanted to see New York."

"I probably won't have room for guests."

"New York. The city that never sleeps."

"Yea, sleeping arrangements might be tough."

"They say it's the greatest city in the world."

"I'll give you a call after I settle in."

"At least hold onto this." She pulls a picture out of her purse. "Look at it when you miss me." It is a picture of Dangie sitting on a large rock in front of a lake.

Exchanging Pleasantries

A clanging sound is heard up the block. Dangie looks to MC and MC to Dangie. "The Angel of lost parts." They both announce together.

An old blue Buick comes creeping down the street. Some backfires are heard. A closer look reveals two different color blue paints, bald tires, no side view mirrors, scuff marks, a missing head lamp, and a dangling license plate.

Behind the steering wheel sits a proud Mort. He believes the sweat he put into the angel of lost parts was worth every long painful minute of the two years he owned the lemon.

Mort rolls down the window which is an effort since he needs vice grips to complete the task. "She's still breathin."

MC coughs and waves his hand in front of his face. "Breathin with emphysema."

"What a you say, one last ride for the city boy before his departure?"

MC and Dangie climb into the wreck. A large puff of smoke blows from the tail pipe.

CHAPTER FOUR

In downtown Manhattan smoke flows steady from a manhole in the middle of the avenue. A constant stream of yellow cabs drive through the cloud and continue to the next traffic light. A policeman waves the automobiles past the blank signal.

A crowd forms on the corner waiting to cross the avenue. Three white boys' ages twelve to thirteen decide to run between the cars. The policeman hollers, he is unable to leave his post to begin a chase.

The boys laugh and continue to run. The smallest of the three turns around to give the officer a look at his middle finger. The officer takes two steps forward wanting to catch the kid and put a scare into him, however, he understands that would be a losing battle.

The boy turns around to hurry along as he slams directly into a large three hundred pound woman in a flowery dress. He hits the floor as the other two boys pause to laugh harder than they ever laughed before.

At first the woman clenches her pocket book in fear of it being stolen. When she notices all of the laughter she feels she is the brunt of a joke and swings the pocket book at the red-faced boy. She misses and some of her belongings fly out of the bag.

Exchanging Pleasantries

Embarrassed, she bends down to pick up the items while the boys catch their breath and continue to run. The police officer has a semi-satisfied grin on his face.

The boys finally come to a stop. They are standing in front of the Marigold Café.

One of the taller boys looks to the shortest of the group. "Whatta ya say Cletta, steal a drink to get refreshed?"

"Let's check it out." Even though Cletta is the smallest of the group, the other two look up to him. Due to the fact that he lives on the streets he teaches the other two how to fend for themselves.

They enter the Marigold Café. Some of the customers become quiet. They are surprised to see children in a coffee shop. Others like Ned continue typing away as if in the middle of a days work.

As usual Ned takes up two tables and has his belongings sprawled around. He's in mid conversation on his cell phone and acts as if he wants the whole café to know his business. "Yes, oh yes. I just finished crushing another dream. Wait till this amateur reads my review of his rubbish." He proclaims himself a writer and belongs to a website where he destroys real writer's hopes of ever becoming published.

The idea of the site is for writers to have a place to bounce ideas off each other in hopes of creating constructive criticism that all parties will benefit

ferf ziamond

from. Ned enjoys spewing his insults instead. "What's another word for extremely bored?" He waits for an answer as Cletta stands nearby at the exotic cookie display waiting for heads to turn away.

"That's it!" Ned hollers as everyone grants him their attention. "I am exceedingly depleted. The ramblings from page one to page twenty-one exasperated my every ounce of energy." As he finishes up his verbal abuse, Cletta pockets a package of the cookies without anyone noticing. He makes his way over to the refrigerator where the other two boys glance at the variety of cold coffee's, overpriced waters, and pastries.

A beautiful young woman in her early thirties approaches them. "Can I give you any assistance gentlemen?" She is the shop manager, Monique.

Cletta grips the cookies in his pocket. "You sure can." He is obviously smitten by her good looks.

"Okay little man, you can take it back out on the street now." She is polite although displeased with their presence.

Cletta makes his way toward the exit as the other two follow. "Could you show us your boobs first?" Cletta walks a little faster expecting anger from the woman. Most of the patrons look on in disgust. A random coffee drinker lets out a slight chuckle.

"That's enough. Keep walking." She walks behind them as they make their way back

Exchanging Pleasantries

to the sidewalk. The door shuts and their laughter can be heard from inside.

Frustrated and slightly amused, Monique walks toward a smiling Dabni at the counter. "You handled that well."

"Not as well as I would have liked to."

"I guess you have to cut some slack to children these days."

"I'd like to cut more than slack on that little wise ass."

CHAPTER FIVE

In front of MC's house, Mort's angel of lost parts sits with the engine turned off while still clunking and clanging with light smoke blowing from under the hood. MC's red Mazda is close by in front. It is filled with bags and boxes.

MC places a final box in the back seat as Mort and Dangie look on. "Well, I guess this is so long for now." MC looks inside the pet carrier on the passenger seat. The eyes of Ferf are peeping from the darkness.

Dangie is holding back tears. She pulls MC close and holds onto him with her arms across his back. "You take care of yourself." She sniffs. "And call us. Even if it means using your Boston Herald phone." She takes a step back to allow Mort to say his piece.

Mort shakes his hand. "Later man."

MC pulls him in closer and puts one arm around him. "It's been a load of laughs." He walks around the car to the driver's side.

He pulls away as his hand sticks out of the window waving. Cutting it short was part of his plan. No tears, no time for deep flowing emotions. His mom and dad are seen at the front window with their arms around each other. Mort looks to them, smiles, and then back at Dangie.

The red Mazda gets further down the road and becomes out of eyes reach.

Exchanging Pleasantries

Dangie stares at Mort. Mort stares back at Dangie. They both look like they want to say something.

The red Mazda makes its way to the highway on ramp. Music plays softly as MC watches the road while talking to himself. "I had to tell them I was called. It's the only way I could have left with any pride." He grips onto the steering wheel.

He told Mort, Dangie and his family that he was heading to New York to write for New York Newsday. That was a lie. In actuality his little office job had a relocation offer that he couldn't refuse. A raise, a months paid rent in an upscale apartment complex, and a chance to experience city life.

MC feels his dream of writing is more of a fairy tale and that he should get off his rear and make some sort of a future for himself. Maybe New York is the place to discover whatever it is that he needs to discover.

The music continues to play softly on the radio. "This is my chance to lie about my life in a positive way. Maybe Newsday will give me a shot after all." Before hitting the road he sent résumé's around to various New York newspapers and magazines. He hoped for a response, deep down inside he didn't expect one though.

He sings along with the music while passing pastures, herds of cows, horse

ferf ziamond

ranches, farms, and a house off in the distance every few miles.

He glances out the passenger side window at the cows and does a quick impression. "Moooooooooo!" He chuckles.

Ferf is becoming restless. "You like that Ferf?"

He taps the pet carrier. Ferf's cries become louder and louder.

Darkness falls. The white lines on the highway are all that is visible under an abnormally large moon.

CHAPTER SIX

Just as the sun rises Monique opens the Marigold Café. A heavy set African American woman with a friendly smile is the first customer of the day. She makes her way to a table as MC'S car pulls up outside the window.

Monique brings the woman a piping hot cup of coffee as MC stretches and yawns before walking up to the entrance.

"Here you go Maisy." Monique places the cup in front of her. "Careful. It's hot."

"Thanks Mo." Maisy opens her newspaper. "I may need your umbrella again hun. It looks like the clouds are coming back again."

"No problem."

Dabni straightens out the counter and runs around making sure all of the coffee pots are set up correctly. The sounds of brewing coffee and the smell of over twenty flavors combined smacks MC in the face as he walks through the door.

Monique grabs a newspaper and heads to her office. She winks at Dabni. "Go easy on him. He looks like an out of towner."

Dabni smiles as Monique enters her office. "Good morning. Welcome to the Marigold Café. May I help you?" She gives MC a big smile.

MC continues to stare at the office door in hopes that Monique will come back out. He is mesmerized by the slight glimpse he had of her. "Uh, yea, I think so." He

ferf ziamond

seems dumbfounded. "Regular, cream and sugar."

Dabni seems a little confused. "Sure, what flavor?"

"Flavor? Coffee. You said this is a café, right?"

"I know coffee but what kind? We have lattes, coolatas, Mocha chinos, Cremalinas, frappaccinos, creamy dippen frattas."

"I don't understand. What is all of that?"

Dabni tilts her head to the side and smiles. She has a cute look. "Monique said you were an out of towner."

MC's face lights up with excitement. "Who's Monique? The woman that went in the back?"

"Yes, that's the manager, Monique. The thirty one year old princess of the East side." She looks to the office door and then back at MC. "So out of towner, where you from?" She pours a cup of a regular form of coffee. The most regular she can find.

MC continues to stare at the office door. "You probably never heard of it. Beverly Massachusetts. Up north. We have regular coffee up in those parts."

She hands him the smoking cup. "This is as regular as we get here. Lemme know if it needs more cream or sugar."

He takes a small sip. "It's good." He blows on the cup to cool it off. "Different, but good."

Exchanging Pleasantries

"So, what do you do in Beverly Massachusetts?"

"That's what brought me here to New York. My company has an office way up north that is downsizing. They offered me an incredible deal to come down here. I had to take it."

"I guess you're very valuable to the company."

"I don't know if I'd say that."

"They seem to have wanted to keep you." She has a convincing tone.

At first MC has a happy, proud look. Then it becomes doubtful. "Unless it was a mistake."

"So, I have family near Boston. They call to scare me sometimes. My mom can't seem to hold a coffee cup like she used to." She catches herself blabbing. "Sorry, sometimes I just keep yapping if no one stops me."

"No. I like it. You're a good yapper."

"Sometimes when I miss her I'll send some refrigerator magnets or kitchen ornaments. See? There I go again. So how far is Beverly from Boston? My dad and I probably pass it on our trips to Maine."

His eyes bulge a bit. "It's quite a hike north of Boston." He looks proud. "I know Boston though. I'm trying to get a job at the Herald."

"Photographer?"

"No writer." He grins. "Well, part time, hoping to become a writer."

ferf ziamond

"Oh, you should meet." She pauses. "Oh never mind."

"Meet who?"

"I just thought of a guy Ned that spends his life here. He's a writer, but the girls seem to dislike him." She makes a familiar face.

"You just reminded me of a friend of mine, Dangie."

"How funny, my name is Dabni."

"Isn't that something?" He looks back at the office door. "Well, her name is actually Angie. I just called her damn Angie so many times that Dangie became her name."

"That's funny."

The office door suddenly opens a crack. MC becomes excited to get another glance at Monique. "Ann here yet Dabni?"

Dabni looks out the window, MC's car can be seen. On the corner across the street Ann is standing waiting for the light to change. "She's right across the street."

"Okay, the rush should be beginning soon." Monique sticks her head out.

MC looks frozen. The moment he waited for from the time he entered the Marigold Café had come. "Uh." He waves. Her face is the most beautiful he's ever seen.

Monique gives a wiggling finger wave to him. "How ya doing doll?" She steps back into the office as MC continues to stare at the door. A few customers make their way in. Ann follows.

Exchanging Pleasantries

"Good morning Ann. Monique was asking for you."

"I know. I'm five minutes late again."

"By the way, this is." Dabni looks over at MC who can't keep his eyes off of the office door. "I'm sorry. I didn't get your name."

He comes out of his trance and looks back at Dabni. "Sorry? Monique?"

"No, your name."

"Oh, I'm sorry. It's MC." He smiles at Ann who is putting on an apron.

"So, whatta you do for fun up north?" Dabni counts out some singles from the register.

"Funny but we spent most our time around a coffee place up there too." He laughs slightly. "The shack it's called."

Dabni smiles at him while in the middle of counting with her lips moving. "Oh yea?"

MC leans on the counter. "Not as fancy as your place. Or should I say Monique's place?" He can't help but smile when saying her name. "I used to belong to an organization called Tag Along."

"What's that?"

"I would act like a big brother or older cousin to a kid. His name is Francis."

"Oh, like Big Brother."

"Yea, that's what I said."

"No, you said like a, big brother. Not Big Brother."

"What's your point?"

25

ferf ziamond

"There is an organization down here called Big Brother. You help nurture kids who don't have any family."

"That's what Tag Along is."

"Glad we established that." She lets out a small laugh. "I belong to Big Sister."

"I guess that's the girl's version." He's obviously being cute.

"Funny." She is amused. "You should look into it down here."

"I would, but what if they give me a black kid?" He has fear in his eyes. The words escaped before he could stop them. All of Grump's prejudice had an impact on him. Some of the customers have blank stares on their faces. Maisy cannot take her eyes off of MC. Her mouth is wide open and she wants to say something. Nothing comes out.

"Excuse me?" Dabni answers in an upset manner.

"I gotta check on my cat." He walks to the door as everyone watches him leave.

He walks out and holds the door for Ned who enters.

CHAPTER SEVEN

MC walks through a revolving door into a lavish and luxurious New York City apartment building. With pet carrier in hand, his eyes bulge and take in all of the sights the lobby has to offer. Chandeliers, bell boys, gold luggage carriers, a four story ceiling with two stairways circling an elevator. His walk to the front desk seems like a hike.

A pretty blonde woman with half a smile greets him at the end of the journey. "May I help you?"

MC puts the pet carrier down. Ferf is a little calmer than in the car, but still loud and disturbing. "Shhhhh. We'll be home in a minute." He pulls out his work ID and apartment paperwork. "Yes ma'am. My job made arrangements for me here."

As the woman snickers and hands the papers back to him she puts two fingers over her mouth. "This is not where they made the arrangements. I'm sorry."

He has a confused look. "No?"

"What you want to do is go two blocks south." She points in that direction. MC studies her eyes.

"Make a left, and it is on the next corner. It's the Brolstar, not the Borellis."

He takes the papers back. "Sorry. My mistake." He makes his way out of the Borellis and hears her voice from behind.

ferf ziamond

"Have a nice evening."

He waves a hand up while approaching the revolving doors.

Out on the street it feels a bit colder. MC zips his jacket up. His car is down the block. It is in the only place he could find a spot, near a homeless shelter. "I better leave the car there. I'm not searching for a spot for another hour and a half."

Annoyed by the New York City lack of street parking, he walks the two blocks south. At the next corner a homeless man stops him asking for change. The man wears rags. He can barely complete a sentence. "Pom a dollar. Pom a quarter. Bar since. Car a home."

MC places Ferf's carrier on the ground and pulls a few bills out of his pocket. "I'd like to give you two dollars but I only have a single and a couple of fives. I don't suppose you have any change?"

The man just stares at MC as if he does not belong in the city. MC stares back for a moment. He looks down at the money. He hands over a five.

"Mmmm, non pel. Dank you." The man makes some noises and MC hurries off. He finds himself under an awning that reads, THE BROLSTAR.

The check in runs smooth. Moments later MC sits on a large bed staring at Ferf who is finally out of his carrier. "It was a rough ride boy." He takes a closer look at the cat. "Girl. Whatever you are."

Ferf jumps off of the bed. The three room apartment appears to be more than the two of them need. Fine oak furniture, a large ceiling fan, modernized kitchen, a fifth floor balcony. "I won't take you in the car ever again. I promise."

MC falls back on the bed. His hands cover his eyes and slowly move down to his mouth and chin. "I can't believe how stupid I was at that café." He reprimands himself. "What a fool I am. How could I talk down about black people when I never really got to know one of them? It's all that idiot Grumps fault." He points the remote control at the television to raise the volume of the football game.

"Football. Maybe I should join that Big Brother thing. I could start fresh with another kid like Francis. We could throw a football around." He turns to the side. The sound of the game can be heard as he closes his eyes. "Big Brother organization." He mumbles to himself.

There is the sound of a long *swoosh*, as if a ball is being sucked through a vacuum chute. The *swoosh* is followed by a young boys voice. "Not what you were expecting?"

MC and a twelve year old African American child are seen standing side by side. Only their heads turn to speak to one another, they never make eye contact. MC is taken aback by the boy's appearance. "You're the one assigned to me?"

ferf ziamond

They appear to be walking down the middle of a busy New York street, almost gliding. A restaurant called QUERO GLEANO, other store fronts, moving vehicles, and other pedestrians drift past them. The only sound is their two voices until the homeless man appears on a corner counting five dollar bills and making noises. "Mmmm, non pel. Dank you. Pom a dollar. Pom a quarter. Bar since. Car a home"

MC looks down toward the boy. "No, not exactly what I was expecting."

"Cause I'm black!"

"You are black."

"It's African American asshole!"

"I apologize."

"You think we coloreds are good at football. That's all we're good for right?" The boy becomes angry. "Well you can blow it out your fat white."

MC is awakened by a referee's whistle on the television. "Damn that Grump." MC rolls over again.

CHAPTER EIGHT

Later in the day at the coffee shack in Beverly, Kamptin walks away from Harper and Grumps table after bringing them two cups of coffee. They are in the middle of a game of checkers. Harper thanks Kamptin then stares out the window at Ludlum Avenue. Grumps eyes continue to open and shut.

The door chimes ring as Mort and Dangie walk in together. Mort is laughing. "Yea, he would have liked that. Writers wanted." He refers to something they read in the newspaper that would have been of interest to MC.

Harper takes his attention away from the window and watches the two of them speaking to Kamptin who hands them each a cup of coffee. Mort pays and they walk towards Harper and Grump. "Who's winning?" Dangie smiles at them.

"I probably am. I can't even tell if he's awake." Harper nods in Grump's direction.

Mort looks at Grump. "He's smarter when he's sleeping anyway."

"Where's Gladstone? He not traveling in your circles anymore?"

"He's a big city boy now. Remember? He took off for New York."

Harper thinks for a moment. "That's right."

Grumps eyes open and he looks at Mort. "Them black kids eat him up yet?"

ferf ziamond

"He lives!" Mort adds some sarcasm.

Dangie can't help being polite. "We haven't spoken to him since he left, but I'm sure no one has given him a hard time."

Grump laughs lightly. "Give it a little time. Them black kids'll get him." He is insistent.

Mort dismisses the comment and sits down at the table two back. Dangie follows after smiling at the men. She takes the seat directly across from Mort and looks deep into his eyes.

CHAPTER NINE

Early in the New York morning before the sun comes up, MC sits on the subway for the first time in his life. He has on a suit, tie, and sneakers that do not go with the ensemble.

There are only two others in the subway car. One, a business man also in a suit, he however wears a pair of dress shoes. The second, an older woman, close to Harper and Grump in age. She is dressed in rags like the homeless man. She has a pushcart in front of her.

Desperately wanting to learn his way around on the subway, MC chooses the business man to ask for tips. "This thing going near Wall Street?"

The man lifts his eyes over his newspaper. After a moments pause he mumbles. "Ten more stops or so."

"Thanks."

"Uh huh."

MC whispers to himself. "Not as friendly as up north."

At the next stop, another train pulls up heading in the same direction. It is the express. MC has no clue what that means. The business man jumps up quickly. He exits MC's train and hurries for the one across the platform. The older woman also gets off at the same stop. She doesn't take the express. She walks slowly down a stairway. Now MC is alone with a nervous feeling.

ferf ziamond

Two young, African American teenage boys, Karu'l and James, get on and look at MC. They can tell he is a stranger to the subway. Karu'l mumbles with his hand over his mouth to James. "Boy must be lost or something." They both laugh loudly and James opens the sliding door leading to the next car. They exit MC's car.

MC becomes very frightened, yet relieved that they moved on. Again he whispers to himself. "Maybe I should have taken Grump more seriously. These black kids may want to kill me." He stares at the sliding door as it opens once again.

In walks Cletta and his two buddies. The three of them stop in front of MC and stare him down. He is still nervous from Karu'l and James and doesn't know what to say.

Cletta slaps one of his friends in the chest. "What's this clown doing in our car?"

The friend grabs MC by the shirt and pulls him up. MC makes two fists. Before he can use them the other kid rushes into him and knocks MC'S head against the door causing him to fall down and black out. The three kids become scared. They aren't sure what to do.

One of them kneels down and fumbles through MC's pockets and grabs his wallet. Cletta decides it is time to get away from the scene. "Drop that and lets move." He heads to the sliding door as the others follow. The wallet is tossed next to MC. The cash is gone.

CHAPTER TEN

MC lies in the same position as in the subway car. This time he is on a worn dark green carpet next to a tan sofa equally tattered. A coffee table is off to the side. It seems to have the same appearance as the wood from the coffee shack. MC's eyes begin to blink open and shut. From a blur, two faces begin to come into focus. They are Karu'l and James.

MC's face is pale and overcome with fear. "No please! Don't kill me! Please!" He yells loudly begging for his life just as Grump said he would.

An older African American man comes running in from another room. He stops and stares down at MC. "See. I told you boys he ain't dead." The man laughs and puts his hand out to help MC up to his feet. While still holding his hand, the man introduces himself. "Carter Bell. Welcome to our home." His smile is warm and hospitable. "These my boys. Karu'l and James."

MC trembles when the young men extend their hands. "You ain't gonna kill me, right?"

Carter puts his hands on his hips. He smiles and then has an annoyed look on his face. "Why would we kill you boy?"

MC looks at the man with fear. He stutters for a moment. "J-just something an old man from back home said about bl-." He stops himself.

ferf ziamond

"Where you from boy?"

"Beverley Massachusetts sir."

"They still got prejudice up there? That's not supposed to be."

"I guess you can say that. They are two harmless old men though."

Carter takes a seat on the tan sofa, he extends his hand for MC to take the seat next to him. "Have a drink son?"

MC is surprised. "Who me?"

"Karu'l lemme have a gin." Carter waves his son on into the kitchen. "Yes you."

"I guess I'll have a glass of water."

"Karu'l, make that two gins." He turns to MC. "I know what happened." Carter appears friendly. He places his hand on top of MC's. "Some old fool told you that the colored folk will get ya. Let me tell you something. It ain't the colored folk that'll get ya, hell, it ain't the white folk that'll get ya either. It's not the Chinese, the Arab, the Muslim, the Jew folk. It's the rotten folk and the rotton folk only that'll get ya. And them folk come in all flavors. You gotta be wise enough to see under the wrapper boy."

MC just stares mesmerized by the words. Karu'l sets two glasses of gin down on the ragged coffee table and leaves the room with his brother.

Carter looks at MC. He can tell he made a new friend. "You got some place to be boy?"

MC continues to stare. "Carter? That's the same name as Carter Bend. Vince

Exchanging Pleasantries

Carter." The words just fall out of his mouth without any explanation.

"What you know about Vince Carter?"

"Just that they named a road and a statue after him."

"I figured as much." He has a disappointed look. "Vince Carter built something. Built something amazing. As years pass, amazing turns into forgetfulness. My daddy didn't forget. He named me Carter for a reason."

MC returns to Carter's previous question. "I guess I should be getting to work."

"Where's that?"

CHAPTER ELEVEN

MC sits in an office cubicle. The walls are a bluish grey. A black computer, matching phone, calculator, and pencil tin sit atop his metallic shined desk. He pulls a small calendar off of the wall held by a push pin and proceeds to cross off the first day of September with a slash mark. He writes across the boxes of the last two weeks in big letters. "FIND AN APARTMENT."

A large man in a suit stands over him.

"Not a big deal that you're late. I'm surprised you made it at all." The man shakes his head while letting out a short cackle. He has somewhat of a box head with short hair and glasses.

MC taps his pen on the computer unit. "What would you like me to begin with Mr. Gohnz?"

Mr. Gohnz steps back. "We're just going to give you some space to get yourself settled today." He continues to walk off. "Call me if you need me." He takes another four or five steps before an attractive young woman hurries over to him flapping pages in front of his face.

MC leans back. "Wow, another one." He is impressed by most of the women he has seen so far. He picks up his phone and dials. At the same time he is logging on to his favorite website.

Exchanging Pleasantries

MC's eyes raise as the phone stops ringing. "Hey Mort!"

Mort sits in his sloppy apartment at a desk on the phone. His sneaker covered feet are up on the desk. A photo of Mort, MC, and Dangie as children is on a night stand. Mort appears to be lounging. Clothes are draped over chairs and an exercise machine. A pizza box lies on his bed. Sun shines through his window, the shade sits raveled on a dresser. "MC? HOLY COW!" Excitement in his voice. "How is the big city boy?"

MC sits swinging his swivel chair back and forth. "I don't know where to begin. So much happened on my first day. Let me just say that the ladies are incredible."

"It makes me real happy to hear you say that." Mort has a tremendous grin. "In love again?"

"No, but this one girl at the coffee shop, she is the most beautiful woman I've ever seen."

"Every woman is the most beautiful woman you've ever seen."

"No, the one that served me wasn't. She was cute, but she was no Monique."

"Monique?"

"Yes, Monique. The manager. She's thirty one, has an apartment on the east side, she likes."

"Oh, yea, you're not in love again."

MC chuckles. "I also had a mishap on the subway."

ferf ziamond

Mort becomes concerned. "Uh-oh. Did Grump put a jinx on you?"

MC is distracted by what he reads on his computer. "You son of a."

"What?"

He changes the subject. "Remember that website I entered some of my writing on?"

Mort comes off with a bit of a sarcastic tone. "How could I forget?"

MC has a look of disappointment. "Oh yea, you rather not discuss my writing."

Mort leans his head back and then pretends to care. "You know I'm just kidding. What happened on the website?"

MC reads quickly to himself the words on the screen. He changes his mind. He'd rather not share his sad news. "It's nothing. Don't worry about it. Just seems like some guy wasn't so impressed by one of my short stories."

Mort feels he has to pretend a bit more. "Oh c'mon, I'm sorry. What'd the asshole say?" A buzz is heard. It's Mort's doorbell. "Oh shoot. Who could that be?"

"The door?"

"Yea, I wasn't expecting anyone." He takes his feet off of the desk.

MC feels it is a quick escape from sharing the review of his story. "Go get it. I have work to get to anyway."

Mort is pleased. "Really? Okay man. Take it easy." Mort quickly hangs up and walks to the door and opens it. Dangie stands there as cute as can be. They both soak each other in for a moment.

Exchanging Pleasantries

MC stares at his computer screen whispering a paragraph. "I am exceedingly depleted. The ramblings from page one to page twenty-one exasperated my every ounce of energy. The catastrophic disarray entitled *Sirens in the sky* is nothing short of a jumble of muddled unintelligible situations rolled into a major disaster."

A tear falls from MC's cheek. He quickly signs off of the computer as his hands shake. He musters up a trifle of energy to get from his desk to the men's room.

Dangie sits at Mort's desk as Mort rubs her shoulders. Her eyes are shut and her smile is gleaming.

Mort hesitates, and then speaks. "That was MC on the phone."

She opens her eyes, looks excited, pauses, and then acts cool. "Oh yea. How is he doing?"

"He got some feedback on his writing."

"How was it?"

"Not sure. That's when you came in."

"How did he sound?"

"He's not gonna make it down there."

Dangie seems concerned and protective. "Aw, that's mean."

A jealous streak crosses Mort. "Whatta ya still have a thing for him?"

Dangie changes the subject. "Let's get a cup at the shack."

Mort throws his denim jacket over her shoulders. "Sure."

CHAPTER TWELVE

MC stands in front of the Marigold Café peeping through the window. He decided to take a walk away from his office and computer.

Inside he sees Dabni organizing coffee pots and pastries. "No Maisy. I guess it's safe to go in." He refers to the large woman he insulted during his last visit.

He walks in the door. Dabni takes one look at him. "Oh you." She is not pleased.

MC approaches her. "Please let me explain."

Dabni walks from the counter to a table. She sprays it and wipes it with some paper towels. "Explain that you are a racist?"

MC steps closer and puts his hand on the spray bottle. "Maybe it looked like that. It's just that someone from up north drilled some negative thoughts about certain people in my head before I came down here." He holds the spray bottle. Dabni lets go.

She looks into his eyes. "Up north huh?"

"Your home town too."

"It's beautiful, but some people are set in their ways. I know how that can be."

MC has a look of relief. "So, this Big Brother organization. Where can I find it?"

Exchanging Pleasantries

Dabni pulls out her pad and pen. They sit. "It's simple." She begins to write as the door opens. Maisy walks in.

"Hi Dabni." She takes a closer look at the two of them. "Oh, it's Mr. Klux of the Klan."

MC quickly stands up. "Maisy. I'm awfully sorry. See, I'm new in town and."

She cuts him off. "Save it Klux. I'm just here to return Monique's umbrella." She places the umbrella next to the counter and turns back around for the door.

MC tries once again to apologize. Before he can get a word out Maisy holds up her hand. "You heard me." She walks out.

MC sits back down across from Dabni. "I wish there was something I could do."

Dabni shows her cute smile. "She likes Fief Te' Loo."

"Who's he? A chef?"

"It's a perfume silly."

"Oh, I thought I smelled something."

Dabni laughs. MC didn't mean to be funny. She looks closer at him for a moment and then directs his attention back down to where she's writing. "What you want to do is take this Avenue right here."

CHAPTER THIRTEEN

Cletta sits at a sloppy desk in a Brooklyn police station. His face has some dirt marks on it and his shirt is torn. An unshaved, annoyed police officer sits across from him. His tag reads, DeMeeco. "You're not as lucky as your buddies. No mom and dad to come down and bail you out." He smirks while jotting down some notes.

Cletta attempts to sound hard. "You can't keep me here." A man walks by in cuffs with two officers shoving him along. He is at the brink of tears. Cletta's eyes follow every step. He becomes humbled and horror stricken. "Can you?"

DeMeeco appears triumphant. "We can't. But we'll hold you until they get here."

"Who are they?"

DeMeeco laughs.

CHAPTER FOURTEEN

Back downtown MC holds the piece of paper given to him by Dabni. Both of his hands grip the edges as he stands on the sidewalk in front of a building. He looks at the paper. 24442. He looks at the building, 24442. Again at the paper, BIG BROTHER. Again at the building, a sign in the window reads, BE A BIG BROTHER. Another says, EVERYONE NEEDS A COMPANION.

MC walks in. A woman behind the desk greets him. Her tag reads, TANYA. "Hello sir. What can I do for you today?" She is pleasant.

MC looks around the office and then at Tanya's silk blouse. "That is a beautiful shirt."

She is taken aback for a moment and then gives him a smile. "Thanks. It's a blouse though. Not a shirt."

"Oh, sorry."

"That's fine."

MC looks at one of the posters behind Tanya. It is a small boy, a puppy, and a father figure all running in a field of grass. The boy is holding a kite string. "I'm from up north. I used to belong to an organization called Tag Along."

Tanya smiles. She knows of the organization. "Oh, up in Massachusetts, right?"

"That's the one."

"So, are you interested in participating in Big Brother of New York?"

ferf ziamond

"That's why I'm here."

Tanya explains how the organization works and waits for MC to produce his ID. "MC, I have to run a background check. Some people like to do this to meet young boys." She has a disgusted look. "As sickening as that may sound."

"I understand." He thinks to himself for a moment. "Actually, I don't understand." A concerned look overtakes him. "I don't understand why they keep sending those kinds of people to overstuffed jail cells when there is so much room at the bottom of the ocean."

Without words, her face shows complete agreement.

CHAPTER FIFTEEN

In a dimly lit, cement walled basement room Cletta sits on a raunchy, splintered, wooden bench in the same Brooklyn police station. There are no bars, just a heavy steel door with an eight by eight inch window. He stares at his fingers in anticipation. His nails are bitten down as far as they can get.

DeMeeco's face appears in the small window. He watches for a moment and then grins. The sound of a key and the turn of a knob bring Cletta to his feet. DeMeeco enters.

They look at one another. "They're upstairs." DeMeeco sounds low in tone. They walk out together.

Upstairs at the same desk Cletta sat at hours earlier sits a woman in a business suit, her hair in a bun. "Hello young man." The woman is from social services.

Cletta is humbled. "Hello ma'am."

She smiles and puts out her hand. "You can call me MS. Garraniet. I will be making a file for you down at my office."

All of the ways he can make fun of her last name consumes Cletta's mind. He controls the urge. "I'm Cletta." He shakes her hand.

CHAPTER SIXTEEN

MC sits in his new apartment on his computer while watching Ferf dart around the room. The moon is big and bright, shining in the sliding glass door along side of his desk. Some of the taller buildings can also be seen from the balcony.

MC reads a note from another member of what used to be his favorite web-site. "MC, I cannot thank you enough for the kind words you used to describe my simple short synopsis of a day in Guadalajara. Yours were the kindest. I almost threw my hopes of writing in the trash can along with my admiration of this web-site after one overly critical note and one unnecessary mauling of my work. Anyway, I just wanted to say THANKS. Josene."

MC has a proud and sympathetic look. "Wow, deep. I'm not alone." He begins to talk softly to himself while typing away a response. "Josene, your work deserved a flattering note. It is obvious you put time and effort in to spilling your feelings on paper as you did. Even if your trip was not the main interest of another reader, someone like myself takes the time to fall deep into your journey to become part of it. I did enjoy it. If I didn't I certainly wouldn't maul it. It appears that this site attracts a small percentage of immature writers who eradicate works like ours in hopes of making theirs seem

Exchanging Pleasantries

better. Yes, I was slammed also, and if you have time, read "Sirens in the Sky" and let me know if you think I received a fair assessment. Thanks MC."

Ferf is finally tuckered out and sprawled on the bed. "Good idea little guy, girl, whatever." MC lies next to Ferf, flips on the television and closes his eyes.

Once again there is the sound of a long *swoosh*, as if a ball is being sucked through a vacuum chute. The *swoosh* is followed by that same Dream child's voice. "Second thoughts Grump?"

Just like the night before, they appear to be walking down the middle of a busy New York street, almost gliding. The restaurant called QUERO GLEANO, other store fronts, moving vehicles, and other pedestrians drift past them. The only sound is their two voices. "I'm not Grump. I left him back in Beverly." MC looks scared.

"You sounded just like him at the Marigold, Klux."

"Have you been speaking to Maisy?"

"Nope." Dream child sounds distant. They still do not make eye contact.

"Carter? Karu'l? James?"

"Those are some people you should be a friend to. Carter can sense things boy. Did you realize they are black?"

"Yes. I know they're black."

"It's African American asshole!"

MC notices Dabni standing in front of a nameless coffee shop. He warns Dream child to be nice. "She is special. Don't say the wrong thing."

"I got ya lover boy."

"I'm serious." MC walks in front of Dabni. The wind blows by both of them. His voice is echoed. "Dream child. This is a very good friend of mine. Without her, you and I wouldn't have met." MC looks down at the top of Dream child's head. "What do we say to a lady?"

Dream child smiles. He looks up at MC not making eye contact, then at Dabni. "Get your ass in the kitchen!"

MC is shocked. He runs to cover Dream child's mouth and falls flat on his face. He is startled from his sleep. He rolls over, looks at the television and makes out the picture of a kitchen design show.

CHAPTER SEVENTEEN

Early in the morning, five AM or so, MC walks into the apartment fitness center. He is in wrinkled sweat pants and a sweat shirt that doesn't match. The room is small but well equipped. There are four treadmills, and a number of benches, free weights, and universal exercise machines.

A beautiful and sexy woman named Tee is walking extra fast on one of the treadmills. Her blonde pony tail bounces with each step. An overweight man sits on a bench with a towel around his neck. He is dripping and stained with sweat but doesn't look very active. An overweight woman is picking up her empty drink bottle and walking towards the door. MC soaks it all in, holds the door for the woman who exits, then stares at the beauty queen who is working up quite a sweat. Her shorts hug her well rounded figure.

MC takes the treadmill on the opposite end. He is less than twenty feet away from the beauty. She takes her eyes off of the television in the corner for a short moment to notice MC.

MC glances over at her machine to try to see what the proper settings are. The overweight man notices this and shakes his head with a slight smile.

MC finally gets his machine moving the way he wants it. It is obvious that he

ferf ziamond

hasn't been in a gym for quite a while. He looks at the woman. "Good morning."

She looks back, out of breath, with a slight smile. "Morning."

"That is a beautiful blouse."

Tee shakes her head and smiles. "Thanks." She is wearing a tank top.

The man shakes his head once again as MC stares at the television and thinks to himself. "There has to be something I can strike up a conversation about. Please give me an in." Just as he finishes his thought, the television news goes to a commercial. It is a cat food ad. A large black and white Balinese leaps across the screen and down to the floor to find his Tristies waiting for him. The glamour beauty sees this and smiles.

MC thinks for a moment and then blurts something out. "My cat looks just like him." He knows Ferf looks nothing like the cat, but to get the chance to speak with her he'll say whatever he needs to say.

She can tell instantly what his agenda is. It's hardly the first time some guy tripped over himself to get her to open up. She joins in the game. "Oh really, what's his name?"

MC not expecting a response fumbles over his tongue. "Far." He pauses for just a second. "Ferf. His name is Ferf."

"Oh that's cute. Did you name him?" She feels her thighs to make MC aware that the treadmill is serving its purpose.

Exchanging Pleasantries

Although Dangie helped with the name, MC doesn't want to admit that he even knows another female. "I sure did. Thanks." He is even happier than when he received the smile from Monique.

CHAPTER EIGHTEEN

Mort lies in his bed a few minutes before ten AM. The sun tries to shine in a window with thick curtains. Clothes are scattered, his television is playing cartoons, and his radio is playing some soft rock and roll. The phone suddenly rings and startles him. He picks up his head and looks around with his eyes half open. "What the heck?"

He pushes the blankets off revealing his ripped sweat pants, red socks, and tank top. The phone is just in arms reach. He extends himself to pick it up on the eighth ring. Grogginess consumes his voice. "Hell. Hello?"

MC sits at his office cubicle. He slashes another day off the calendar. His computer screen shows the normal writers website. He taps a pen against a coffee cup. "Sounds like someone had a rough night."

Mort clears his throat. "Hey city boy. What's up in the big apple?"

"What apple?"

"That's what they call New York."

"Who are they?"

"I don't know." He rolls over to put his elbows on the bed to hold himself up. "How's the love life with all the new babes."

"Oh man I'm glad you brought it up." MC's eyes light up. He looks as if he is having a picture perfect dream. "I met the

Exchanging Pleasantries

most gorgeous woman on earth this morning at the gym."

Mort holds back a laugh. "What the hell were you doing at a gym?"

"All right. Very funny. I went there because it is included in my new temporary apartment." He makes a muscle and pokes at it with three fingers. "You wouldn't believe this girl."

"What happened to Mona, or Monica, whatever her name is?"

"Monique. And if it doesn't work out with Tee, I'm still going to try for Monique. But I think Tee likes me."

Mort is slightly sarcastic. "I'm sure she does." His doorbell buzzes. "Oh, I better see who that is."

MC sits while Mr. Gohnz stands over his shoulder. "Yea, you get that. I have a lot of business to attend to." He puts the phone down. "Oh, hello Mr. Gohnz. I didn't see you there." He pretends that he was getting off the phone anyway.

Mort opens his front door. Dangie stands on the opposite side.

Mr. Gohnz is especially nice to MC. "That is quite all right. Stay on the phone as much as you like." He pats MC on the back. "How are you enjoying your new apartment?"

MC feels as if something is up. A boss is not supposed to be so nice to an employee. At least it was never like that at the other office. "It is spectacular. I wish it was permanent."

ferf ziamond

"That would be nice. But before you go looking for something permanent come see me. I know some people."

"Thanks sir. That is awfully nice." MC changes the subject. "Do you have anything for me to do today?"

"Relax kid. Take some time to learn your way around. Don't worry about work. Explore the internet." Mr. Gohnz begins walking back to his office. "Take an extended lunch." He waves his hand over his head. The same attractive young woman hurries over to Mr. Gohnz flapping pages in front of his face once again.

MC spins back around on his chair and reads Josene's response to his note. "Hi MC. It seems you always know what to say. Thanks again. Also, I found "Sirens in the Sky" and I read it. And no, it did not receive a fair assessment. There are some things I would change about it, but all in all I really enjoyed it and it was very well written. So what is your age/status? Josene." He smiles to himself. "Wow, another woman to romance. I should tell her I'm available, but I shouldn't sound desperate." He stops and rests his head on his fist while thinking.

A few minutes later he raises his head and appears to have a plan. "Or, this is an interesting idea." He begins to whisper to himself while typing again. "Hello again Josene. First off, thank you for the comments regarding "Sirens in the Sky". And please, if you think you have ideas for it, give it a re-write and maybe you can enlighten me. As far as my age and status, I came up with something interesting. Tell me how you feel about this. We each write a story. Yours about how you picture me. A day in the life sort of thing. I'll do the same about you. When we're done, we'll put them together. Maybe we could enter it in the contest. MC." He sits back with his arms folded with a look of achievement.

Moments later he pulls out a scrapbook and begins to write some notes.

CHAPTER NINETEEN

Cletta sits at a desk across from Ms. Garraniet. Her office is dimly lit. Two neat stacks of paper sit beside a computer monitor and a phone. Various framed photos of children decorate the book shelf behind her.

She fills out paperwork while he fiddles with a desk ornament, a playground with fake snow circulating as he shakes it. Her glasses sit at the end of her nose as she looks at Cletta. "You're only thirteen and you're attempting to mug undercover subway officers?"

Cletta puts the ornament down and looks at her with sorrowful eyes. "He looked like a bum."

"That doesn't make it any better."

Tanya knocks on the half open door. "Ms. Garraniet? Is this a bad time?"

"No, no. Come right in. He is yours."

She walks over to where Cletta sits nervously. "Hi, you must be Cletta." She offers her hand.

He hesitates then shakes it. "Hi."

Ms. Garraniet introduces them to one another and hands some forms to Tanya.

"We have a big brother waiting for you Cletta."

Cletta looks up at Tanya with a half smile. Deep down he feels that having a big brother is what he needs. Even if it comes as part of a punishment he is wise enough to see the deeper meaning.

CHAPTER TWENTY

Over at the Marigold, Dabni is pouring a cup for Maisy who sits at her usual table. Ned also takes up his usual two tables with his belongings spread out behind them.

Dabni and Maisy are in mid conversation. "No, it's not like I have a thing for him. There is just something appealing about him."

Maisy motions for Dabni to stop pouring. "That's enough girl. I got to get back to work." She looks in Dabni's eyes. "Once a racist, always a racist my daddy taught me."

"Maybe you should give him a chance."

"Mmmmm Hmmmm. I ain't disrespecting my daddy like that. The day I give someone like Klux a chance is the day I have my own umbrella and stop using Monique's. Be a love and give this back to her." Maisy holds up the umbrella once again. "It seems to be clearing up."

"That's another part of it. He has a thing for Monique. He wouldn't give me a second look."

"And Monique wouldn't give him a second look." She lifts herself from the seat. "I'm just gonna run to the ladies room."

Dabni begins wiping the table as Maisy walks toward the back "Once a Klux, always a Klux." She reaches the bathroom door.

MC walks in the front door and towards Dabni. Monique walks out of her office

ferf ziamond

with her eyes glued to a booklet she is reading. MC stares at Monique and becomes very distracted as Dabni turns around and they bump into one another. "Oh Klux!" The cup falls to the ground and coffee is spilled. "I mean MC, sorry."

"Don't you mean klutz?" He bends down to pick up the cup.

Monique looks over angrily at Dabni, then back at her booklet. She pours a cup and turns back toward the office door as Dabni apologizes loud enough for her to hear. "My fault sir."

Monique walks back into her office.

MC feels uncomfortable and thankful at the same time. "That was too nice of you. I should have taken the blame for you. You could get fired, not me."

"Yea, but I know you don't want Monique to think you're a klutz."

"How'd you get that impression?"

She bends down to wipe the floor. "I could just tell."

"You still didn't have to do that."

"No biggie. I've spilled coffee in a few big cities. I still think back home is my favorite place to spill coffee." She smiles. "I suddenly have an urge to call my mom."

MC smiles back. "Speaking of Klutz's and Klux's, I was wondering if you could give this to Maisy next time she comes in." He hands her a small gift wrapped box with a note.

Exchanging Pleasantries

Her smile grows bigger. "Well you're in luck. She's in the ladies room."

MC becomes nervous. "I think I'd rather you did it. I was just stopping by on my way to meet my new little brother and thought I'd let you know since you sorta set it all up."

"I understand. Maybe this will make her get her own umbrella."

MC doesn't understand the comment. He seems to make a mental note of it though.

She takes the box and he rushes out just as Maisy comes from the back.

Ned shakes his head and mumbles to himself. "For God's sake. This is not the easiest place to concentrate. Damn Marigold Mooch again."

"What are you smiling about?" Maisy looks at Dabni as she hands her the gift.

"Someone came to visit you."

"What is this?" She begins reading the note. "I know there is a phrase for when words come out right. I don't know if there is one for when words come out jumbled. Not giving me the time of day has made me more than humbled. I'm trying to be a writer but no-one ever said I was a poet. Please accept this small token as a peace offering." She begins to tear it open and notices it is signed Klux with the K crossed out. "Fief Te' Loo? You had to say something." She appears touched.

"Well? What do you think of him now?"

ferf ziamond

"I'm not that easy. And he didn't even write what the phrase is for when words come out right."

Ned quickly scribbles some notes.

CHAPTER TWENTY ONE

MC walks into the Big Brother office where Cletta now sits in front of the desk facing Tanya. Cletta turns around quickly to see who is walking in. He notices MC and quickly remembers him from the subway. He becomes nervous and afraid.

Tanya stands up. "Right on time MC. I'd like you to meet Cletta, your new little brother."

Cletta's forehead begins to shine with a coat of sweat. He is nervous as they lean in to shake hands. MC looks closely at him with a puzzled face. "Hi. Nice to meet you. You look like someone I met before but I can't seem to place it."

Cletta tries to move his face away so not to be recognized. "I just have one of those faces."

Tanya sits back down and pulls out a small pamphlet. "You just have a couple of forms left to sign MC and then you guys can get acquainted."

MC sits in the chair along side Cletta.

CHAPTER TWENTY TWO

Over at the coffee shack Kamptin is in his usual spot behind the counter rinsing cups and spoons. Harper and Grump stare at their checkerboard with four black pieces in front of Harper, two of which are kings. Grump has six red pieces, one of which is a king.

The chimes ring and in walk Dangie and Mort arm in arm sharing a laugh. "Two of your finest brewed Kamptin." Mort motions for Dangie to take a seat as he pulls out some money.

Kamptin gives Mort a curious look. "Here you go. You guys a couple now?"

Mort lays down three singles on the splintered counter. "We'll see. Keep the change Kamptin." He walks past Harper and Grump on his way to their usual table.

Harper whispers to Grump whose eyes are half shut. "I thought that was Gladstone's girl." He raises his voice towards Mort. "Where the hell is Gladstone anyway?"

Grump is startled. "What? My turn again?"

Mort looks over at them. "He's still in New York."

"Since when?"

"Since last time we told you."

"I can't keep up with you kids."

Grump makes an illegal move on the board. "King me!"

Harper places a black checker on one of his own. "Good move old timer."

Exchanging Pleasantries

"I'm red you fool. I never take black!" He turns to Mort. "Speaking of the blacks, when is Gladstone's funeral?"

"You're a barrel of laughs. You should be back in Vaudeville."

Grump turns back around. "What does that youngster know about Vaudeville?"

Harper stares out the crusty window.

Mort holds onto Dangie's hand and they continue to smile at one another.

CHAPTER TWENTY THREE

The first place MC takes Cletta to is Marigold Café. MC has his hand on the door ready to pull.

Once again Cletta appears nervous. "You really think this is a place for children?"

"C'mon. This is the first place in the city I made any friends. You'll like it."

"I don't know."

"You like girls?"

"Hell yea."

"Well there's one I'd like you to meet."

"Uh oh."

MC opens the door and pushes Cletta softly on the back. "Let's go."

Ned sits in his usual office space. "Oh jeez, the Marigold Mooch again. Time to take more notes."

Ann walks past Ned and looks to MC and Cletta. "I'm surprised you came back here."

"What? My little mistaken comment?"

"Not yours. His." She points to Cletta and then looks to Monique behind the counter. "Monique, your little friend is here."

Monique looks over. "Oh no." She steps out from behind the counter and looks at MC. "If you're going to bring your son in here I expect an apology."

"I'm sorry but he's not my son." MC looks down at Cletta. "Why am I apologizing?"

Exchanging Pleasantries

"Not you. Him. He said something vulgar to me the other day."

"I'm sorry ma'am. That was before my big brother was here."

Monique is satisfied with the apology. She goes back to what she was doing.

"Speaking of Big Brother, where is Dabni?"

Monique has a look of remembrance. "Oh yea, that's right. You're the klutz that caused her and I to have words. She needed some time off." She looks back down.

"Fired?"

"No. I could never fire my best." She pauses and looks at Ann who is waiting for her to continue. "My second best server. She'll be back in a day or two."

Ned is watching while jotting down some notes.

MC takes Cletta by the hand and they walk towards the door. They get outside and MC looks down at him. "Well, that went well."

"Yep."

"What did you say to her?"

"Could you show us your boobs?"

"What did she say?"

"She chased us out."

"A boy after my own heart. And I asked if you like girls. So, who are us?"

"Oh, just two of my friends and me. They have parents. That's why they didn't have to stay at the police station."

"That doesn't sound fair."

ferf ziamond

"Life's not fair." Cletta looks over at MC while they continue walking down the city street. "At least that's what I hear."

MC smiles. "At least you won't have to get your hearing checked. That's right on the money. So, you want to visit some friends I made uptown?"

"Isn't it dangerous uptown?"

"What do I know? I'm a country boy from up north. We just have to find the place. Besides, I have some free time. My boss has been overly generous with giving me time away from the office. Leaving early, long lunches, no projects. It's a big difference from what I'm used to."

"Maybe he has a crush on you." Cletta cracks a smile.

MC slows down. He has a baffled look on his face. "Could that be possible? I've heard about that kind of thing."

CHAPTER TWENTY FOUR

MC and Cletta stand side by side in front of a large steel door labeled 2G. "I know this is the number. I hope it's the right building." MC knocks on the door.

"I don't want to walk on those streets again. Even though I'm a kid from the streets, some of those people looked pretty mean."

"People look how you make them look. If you look at them like you're afraid of them, they're going to appear mean."

Karu'l's voice is heard from inside. "Who's there?"

"It's MC!"

The door opens. "MC who?" Karu'l looks at them. "Oh subway man. How you feelin? Come in." Karu'l shakes MC's hand and pulls him inside. Cletta follows. "Dad! James! Look who's here!"

Carter walks into the living room with a tremendous smile. James follows. Cletta takes it all in. He feels a family warmth as soon as he sees the three men together. Being from the streets makes the run down apartment seem like a castle.

Carter greets MC with a hug. "I'm happy we gave you a good enough feeling for you to return." He looks behind himself. The newspaper is spread out on the couch. "Have a seat. Boys, move them papers." He looks to Cletta. "Who's this?"

MC and Cletta sit next to each other after Karu'l organizes the newspaper.

ferf ziamond

"This is my new little brother. You are the first people I wanted him to meet. Well, besides some girls."

"I can understand that. So can my boys. Right boys?"

Karu'l and James answer at the same time as if it is rehearsed. "Watch how you treat the ladies."

"That's right."

Cletta hopes MC doesn't mention what he said to Monique when he met her. He can tell that Carter is a man of respect.

MC clears Cletta's worry. "That's what I'm teaching my little bro here." He pats Cletta on the back.

Carter enjoys the response. "That's what I wanna hear. Boys. Why don't you show?" He holds his hand out to Cletta.

"Cletta sir."

"Why don't you show Cletta your room?"

Karu'l stands at the refrigerator. "Sure dad. You want a drink first?"

Carter looks to MC. "MC?"

"Sure. I'll have the same as last time."

"Two gins."

"Do you have any crackers in the house?" MC inquires innocently. The boys let out a laugh. Carter gives them a striking look.

James quickly loses his smile and brings Cletta to their room. Cletta's eyes light up. There is a writing desk, a set of bunk beds, two dressers, and a small

Exchanging Pleasantries

table with a television on top. The room is neatly organized without a spec of dust for the eye to see. "So, how old are you Cletta?"

"Thirteen. Wow! You have a TV?" He admires the small black and white television with rabbit ears sticking up from it.

James has a hint of sarcasm. "Yea, we're spoiled."

"I never really watched much TV. I can remember being real young, maybe five or six and there was one in the hospital."

"Why were you in the hospital?"

"I don't know. Just woke up there one day I guess."

"Well, you can watch our TV whenever you like. Say, MC didn't mention he had a brother."

Karu'l enters the room.

MC sits next to Carter in the living room. Carter is speaking. "You have to make a boy like Cletta into a strong self sufficient young man. There are too many wild, obnoxious fools running around out there due to bad parenting. I bring my boys up right. I can't tell you how many times the police had to visit many of the homes of my friends because of their children's disrespect for decency. And you can tell your friend from up north that they were all flavors."

MC watches Carter speak with significant interest. "This is the second time I'm

ferf ziamond

taking on this responsibility. I did Tag Along back up north for a few years."

"You're a good kid. I'm impressed. And I'm not that easy to impress. If you ever need any guidance during the challenge don't hesitate to call."

CHAPTER TWENTY FIVE

At five AM the next morning, MC wakes and hits his alarm clock. He looks into the living room where Cletta is snoring on the couch. MC shakes him lightly. "I'm off to the fitness center. You're welcome to tag along."

Cletta mumbles in his sleep. "What floor is it on? I'll meet you there."

"The second." MC quietly leaves.

MC walks into the fitness center. He is in a different pair of wrinkled sweat pants and another sweat shirt that doesn't match. Everything is like a repeat of his first trip to the gym.

Tee, the same beautiful and sexy woman is walking extra fast on the same treadmill as before. Her blonde pony tail bounces with each step once again. This time she greets MC when he enters. "Good morning."

"Hi Tee. Are you still on that thing?" They share a laugh at his little quip.

The overweight man sits on the bench with a towel around his neck once again. He shakes his head at the joke.

One difference from earlier is another attractive young girl on a stationary bike off to the side. Tee looks over at her. "This is my neighbors little girl, Amanda, we call her Mandy."

Mandy waves to MC.

"Nice to meet you Mandy." He notices that she is pretty but something about

ferf ziamond

her seems young. She is one of those thirteen year old girls who appear to be over seventeen.

MC takes the same treadmill as last time. Just as he gets on, Cletta bangs his arm against the door. His voice is heard from inside. "OUCH!"

MC climbs off of the treadmill to let him in. He opens the door. "You need to swipe a card for the door to open or else you can hurt yourself."

Cletta smirks. "Really?" They both laugh. Cletta stares at Tee for a moment, then at Mandy who is staring back at Cletta. Cletta's eyes then quickly go back to Tee. "Oh man." He whispers.

MC makes the introductions.

On the television the same Tristies commercial is playing. Tee smiles. "Look, it's Ferf!"

MC smiles back then looks to Cletta. "Ferf doesn't look."

MC cuts him off. "So Cletta, why don't you tell the girls how you like Big Brother so far?" He figures while shutting him up he can also make himself look good.

Cletta is obviously cheerful. "There's no one like MC. I wish he came here seven years sooner."

CHAPTER TWENTY SIX

Later on in Beverly, Dangie kneels on Mort's bed in dark blue jeans, a tee shirt, and socks. Mort sits at his desk across from her with his eyes glued to her. Bright sun light glares on the television screen from a window. The room is cleaner than normal.

He slowly makes his way over to where she kneels. He appears giddy, a bit awkward and goofy. "Do you like this show?" He leans over to grab the remote. Dangie places her hand on his chest and their lips slowly meet.

The kiss lasts for close to four seconds when the phone rings startling them both.

Mort seems annoyed as he picks up. "Yea?"

"Hey Mort. Whatcha doin?" MC sits at his cubicle. His normal website is up on his computer.

"Oh, uh, hi MC." Mort looks to Dangie while shrugging his shoulders. "Something important?"

"Nah, just thought I'd say hello."

"Well um."

"Look, I wanted to apologize to you and Dangie."

"It's okay." Mort looks lost.

"Do you know why?"

"No, I guess not." He wants to rush him off the phone. He feels guilty about being with Dangie.

ferf ziamond

"I'm sorry. I totally forgot to give you and Dangie a goodbye gift. You know I never like to leave without giving something."

"It's okay. It's okay."

"Really?"

Dangie begins kissing Mort's neck. He becomes fluttered. "Yea, yea."

"Is this a bad time buddy?"

Mort is no longer paying attention to MC. He leans over for another kiss.

Dangie giggles. "Is he still there? What he say?"

Mort drops the phone. He whispers in Dangie's ear. "Sorry no goodbye gift."

"What?"

"No goodbye gift. MC didn't give us any."

"Oh. He gave me one."

"Really?"

"Yea."

"What?"

"I'm kissing it."

"Oh yea, I guess he gave me one too." They continue to kiss. They knock the photo of Mort, MC, and Dangie to the floor. It drops next to the phone where MC's voice is heard.

"Mort? Mort? Are you messing with me?"

The two of them lay back on the bed.

MC looks at the receiver and smirks. "I hope everything is okay over there." He goes back to the computer screen to read Josene's reply note.

Exchanging Pleasantries

"Hi MC. I went ahead and began my own version of "Sirens in the Sky" like you suggested. I renamed it "Blaring Siren" and I turned your main character Timmy into a fire fighter. I hope you don't mind. I also loved your idea of a day in the life and began writing that as well. Let me know your feelings. Your friend, Josene."

MC does not hesitate a response. "Josene. The fire fighter idea sounds inspiring. Any reason in particular you went with it? I started putting notes together on the day in the life also. Now that I know you like it, I will continue. Talk to you soon. MC."

He clicks the send button and turns around to see Mr. Gohnz standing behind him. "You're doing a marvelous job son."

"Oh, hello Mr. Gohnz. Do you have anything for me to do?"

Mr. Gohnz smiles and rubs his chin. "Why don't you head out a little early and entertain that new little brother of yours?" He begins to walk off.

MC is pleased as well as confused. "Marvelous job? I haven't done anything since I started here." He continues whispering. "A little early? I've only been here a few hours." He begins shutting down his computer and slashes another day off the calendar.

Mr. Gohnz is not too far off in the distance when the same lovely woman confronts him with paperwork. She begins

ferf ziamond

waving it once again and then speaks softly. "How much longer are you going to let this kid go on living away from home to adapt in a place where he has no future?" She appears upset.

He pulls her gently to the side and puts his index finger to his lips. "Shhhhh. Quiet Miss Beowd. I'm still not sure how I'm going to break it to him."

"Well you better do it soon. His paychecks will be ending before long." She walks off in a bit of a huff.

MC turns back around unknowingly from his computer screen and watches her walk off. Mr. Gohnz looks at him with fear that the conversation may have been overheard. He waves gently.

MC looks at him sadly until Mr. Gohnz turns around. MC whispers under his breath. "Maybe he does have a crush on me. That's sick."

CHAPTER TWENTY SEVEN

For the next couple of days, MC continues to make slash marks on his calendar. The last day of the complimentary apartment is approaching quickly.

Harper and Grump sit playing checkers at the coffee shack each day. Mort and Dangie walk in holding hands and laughing appearing happier from one day to the next. Kamptin gives them warm smiles.

MC and Cletta keep up appearances at Carter Bell's apartment. Karu'l and James entertain Cletta in their room on the floor in front of the small television while Carter continues giving MC pointers on raising a respectable young man.

Night after night before falling asleep MC writes in his scrapbook in his dark apartment while Ferf lies next to him.

Dabni continues to try to convince Maisy that MC is not prejudice. They converse at Maisy's table day in and day out at the Marigold Café. Maisy shakes her head back and forth in disagreement when Dabni tries to explain.

Monique looks on from her office. She appears angry about something when noticing Ned who looks on and jots down notes, speaks into a cell phone and types on his laptop.

MC and Cletta keep up their appearances at the gym. They talk and laugh with Tee and Mandy. The overweight man looks on. The Tristies commercial comes on the

ferf ziamond

television now and then and Tee always remarks about Ferf and points to it.

MC, Cletta, Tee, and Mandy begin to see each other away from the gym. They sit at an outdoor table at QUERO GLEANO having lunch. MC opens his wallet. The picture of Dangie stares back at him. He looks sad for a moment and appears to miss her.

Mort and Dangie pull in front of Mort's apartment in the Angel of Lost Parts. She leans over for a kiss.

CHAPTER TWENTY EIGHT

Mr. Gohnz stands with a tear in his eye behind MC who is typing away on his favorite website.

MC notices him and has an important question. "Good morning Mr. Gohnz. I am ready to discuss what you offered a couple of weeks ago."

Mr. Gohnz composes himself. "What is that son?"

"Are you okay?"

"I'll be fine. What is it you wanted to discuss?"

"Remember you said before I go looking for somewhere permanent to live I should come see you because you know some people? Here I am to see you sir." MC appears very happy.

Mr. Gohnz rubs his temple and grunts to himself. "You're not going to make this any easier are you?" He looks over his shoulder and sees Miss Beowd glancing in their direction.

MC's happiness turns to worry.

"Look son." He sits on MC's desk. "There was a mistake."

"I don't understand. I couldn't have made a mistake."

"Not you. Us. You see, the company, actually Miss Beowd, miscalculated the needs during this whole relocation project." He looks over at Miss Beowd once again. She sees that Mr. Gohnz is breaking the news and she walks off.

ferf ziamond

"So my services are no longer needed."

"Unfortunately."

"I understand sir. Actually I'm not surprised."

"That is very big of you MC."

"Now I see why you were so nice to me."

Mr. Gohnz clears his throat. "Yes son. Let me know if you need any help gathering your things."

MC shuts down his computer and throws some items in his Trenis' Times bag. "No. I'm good. I know it's not your fault and you've been great about everything. I'm just sorry I don't have a going away gift for you." MC takes a few steps toward the elevators.

Mr. Gohnz has a crack in his voice. "Just spending the little time we had together was a gift to me."

MC turns around, he looks slightly uncomfortable. He mumbles under his breath. "He can't have a crush on me." He looks at Mr. Gohnz who gives a wink. MC rushes into an elevator that opens up.

CHAPTER TWENTY NINE

MC stands at Carter Bell's door labeled 2G as it opens. Carter can tell immediately that something is wrong. "Why the long face boy?" Carter motions for MC to have a seat while he walks into the kitchen.

"Looks like plans have changed."

Carter pours two gins. "You can't stay here in New York no longer, right?"

"How'd you know?"

"I can sense things boy."

"That's spooky."

Carter puts a glass in front of MC and takes a seat. "I know you say things as innocent as can be but some folks take offense to things like spook or even cracker like you said the other day. It's not your fault. The world has been creating words for one person to insult another since the beginning of time. Before long, words like bunny rabbit or preciousness will have the same affect as saying dammit after God or mother after your. The world is a strange place. A gift gone spoiled."

"At least I'll be taking home some of your wisdom Carter. I wish I had something to give to you and the boys."

Carter laughs. "Boy, you done give us enough. That is as long as you ain't taking Cletta with you."

"Oh no sir. I haven't even thought about that."

ferf ziamond

"He's inside with the boy's right now. They the best of friends since you came around. Karu'l even got the boy work. Look, I love the boy like he's my own. Your short impression on him was magical. If you promise to take on a new tag along back up north, Cletta will be our new little brother."

"You got a deal there Carter."

"You going to that coffee place you been talking about before you leave?"

"I haven't given that much thought either. I guess I have to say goodbye to them over there." He looks upward. "I can't forget about Dabni."

"As much as I am against that over priced yuppie mud-water, me and the boys will come by to say so long."

MC has an unforgettable smile that lights up his face. "That would be a memory to take back home."

Carter puts his sock covered feet up on the coffee table, grins and takes a sip of his gin.

CHAPTER THIRTY

MC wakes up early the next morning. All of his belongings are packed beside his apartment door. He grabs the pet carrier that holds Ferf. "C'mon you genderless prize. We got work to do." They exit the apartment.

MC enters the exercise room. Tee and Mandy are finishing up their workout.

MC is uncomfortable. "Tee. Hi. I want to say something to you."

She approaches him and holds his arm. "Is everything okay?"

"Yes and no. I have to head back home. Up north."

"Oh, that's too bad."

"I wanted to give you a gift. I don't like saying goodbye without giving something." He holds the pet carrier out and opens the door.

Tee almost melts. "Awwww. Is this little Ferf?" She holds Ferf and looks closely at its face. "You said Ferf looked like the cat on TV."

MC becomes shy. "I have an apology." He looks downward. "I couldn't have started a conversation by saying, that cat doesn't look like my cat, could I?"

"No I guess not. So why aren't you taking Ferf back home with you?" She holds Ferf up.

"I sorta promised him no more car trips. It's not nice to break a promise to your cat."

ferf ziamond

Tee holds Ferf up higher.

MC regains courage. "So, maybe we could get together for a date or something if you're ever in my town or I'm ever back in your town?"

She has an apologetic smile. "MC. I like you. I like you a lot. But as a friend. We can stay friends."

He is crushed. He tries to deal with it. "Yea, sure. I was just saying. You know?"

She continues to hold Ferf up while looking underneath, she changes the subject. "Is Ferf a boy or a girl?"

He laughs slightly. "Good question. I'm not sure. My girlfriend picked it out."

Tee lets the girlfriend comment slide by. She realizes it is just a line to help him get over the rejection. "So, Mandy, you have to say goodbye to MC."

Mandy walks over to shake his hand. "Can you guys share Ferf? I didn't bring you anything Mandy."

"Don't worry. You gave me a better gift."

"What was that?"

"I think she has a thing for Cletta."

Mandy smiles.

CHAPTER THIRTY ONE

MC returns to his apartment for one last look around. The phone comes into his vision. "What the hell. One last call, it's on the company." He walks over and dials.

Back in Beverly Mort sits alone in his apartment at his desk. Cartoons are on the television and music plays softly as the phone rings. The photo of Mort, MC, and Dangie is back on the night stand where the phone sits ringing.

He picks it up and hears MC's voice. "Hey! I was just thinking of you. How goes it in the big city?"

"It's not easy. I can remember when everything was simpler. You, me, Dangie, the people on Ludlum Avenue and Carter Bend. Now it's all work, chasing dreams, and mixing positives."

Mort looks at the photo next to the phone. He picks it up and holds it while staring at each young face slowly. "Yea, I guess our moms were right. We do grow up right before their eyes."

MC pulls the phone away for a moment and just looks at it. "Mort? Is that really you?"

"What's wrong?"

"That sounded too deep to be the Mort I know."

"I'm too deep? What the hell is mixing positives?"

ferf ziamond

"I don't know. There's a phrase for what I really want to say. Like when meeting some girl in a gym, in a coffee shop, on a writer's website. Quick blurbs about your days, simple greetings, there's a word for that. Or two words for that."

"You're the writer."

"Not according to some people."

"Still down about those sour comments buddy? I got some news that'll cheer you right up."

"Really? Cause the reason I called was to give you some big news."

"You sound like you need to go first."

"I'm coming back home!"

Mort is shocked. After a moment he speaks. "Well, if you're coming home, my big news can wait till you get here."

CHAPTER THIRTY TWO

MC approaches his car that he hasn't so much as peeked at during his stay in New York City. He opens the car door and the smell smacks him in the face. A bottle or two, crumpled paper bags, and a corroded head of lettuce fall to the street next to his feet.

A snore can be heard coming from the back seat, a closer look reveals the homeless man he met weeks earlier. MC shakes and startles him. "Pom a dollar. Pom a quarter. Bar since. Car a home."

MC smirks. "At least now I know what that last part means."

At the Marigold Café, Ann runs around picking up after customers trying to make it through another morning rush. Dabni is not there and Monique only sticks her head out to check once in a while.

The crowd gets smaller and smaller to reveal Ned taking up his usual space. He is deep in thought and typing away at his laptop.

In walk Carter Bell, Cletta, Karu'l, and James. Cletta knows his way around. He scans the area for Monique. She's no where to be found.

Ned pops his head up for a second, sips his fratte latte, makes a displeased face towards Carter and the family, and resumes his business.

"Shall we take a seat?" Carter looks to Cletta.

ferf ziamond

Just then MC's car pulls up out front. He is snagged by his umbrella getting out. He tries to squeeze it back in with the piles of luggage, it's a no go. He puts the umbrella under his arm with the Trenis' Times bag and walks with it.

MC enters the Marigold. "SURPRISE!" The group lets out an unrehearsed holler.

Ned looks up again. "Oh Lord. The Marigold Mooch is still in town." He lowers his head and tries to block out the commotion.

Ann peers over and smiles. She gives a quick wave. MC reciprocates. She heads toward the coffee pots.

Monique's head pops out to see what the festivities are about. She whispers. "Pssst. Ann. Is that the guy that always bothers Dabni?"

"Yes, but I don't think she would call it a bother."

"What does he want?"

"I think he's just celebrating something with his friends."

Cletta and MC notice Monique at the same time. They both give her a child like grin and wave.

Monique grits her teeth, waves back and continues her conversation with Ann. "I thought he didn't like black people."

"I swear. No one can give the poor guy a chance." Ann brings a regular coffee over to MC. "Here you go hun. Anything for your friends?"

Exchanging Pleasantries

"I'll take these cookies. And I'd like to pay twice if that's all right?" Cletta takes the gourmet cookies off the shelf and holds up a ten dollar bill.

"That would be fine. Just a bit strange." Ann takes the ten and MC follows her to the register.

"Can I ask you something Ann?"

"She quit."

"How'd you know what I was going to ask?"

"Call me a psychic. It wasn't that hard to tell. I know your eyes were on Monique, but I could tell your heart was wrapped up in Dabni."

"Wow."

"Yea, I'm good. So what brings the gang here?"

"I'm heading back home. They're giving me the royal send off."

"Couldn't handle the city life?"

"The city couldn't handle me." He cracks a smile.

"I can see why she was so crazy about you."

"Yea, well, there's always Dangie to settle for back home."

"No one should ever just settle."

"Thanks again for everything Ann."

"You too. And good luck kid." She extends her hand and they shake.

MC returns to the table. First he approaches Cletta. "I guess this is it little brother." They hug.

ferf ziamond

"Thanks for all the new friends big brother. I could never have got on the straight and narrow path without you." Cletta slips the cash that was stolen on the subway into MC's Trenis' Times bag.

MC moves on down the line as Maisy's face can be seen through the window in front of MC's car.

MC holds onto Karu'l's arm with his right hand and James' with his left. Karu'l wipes his eye. "Thanks for the new brother."

"You're a good man MC. Just stay off them subway's." James causes them to laugh.

Carter grabs onto MC especially firm. "You're a special boy. Anything, anytime. The Bell family is always here for ya."

Maisy has to rub her eyes while entering the Marigold. "I can't hardly believe this. You all friends with Kl- I mean Lux here?"

"He's one of the good ones ma'am." Karu'l smiles to Maisy.

She scratches her head. "Maybe Dabni was right." She holds onto MC. "I'm sorry Lux. She is the one for you."

MC hands her his umbrella. "It looks cloudy Maisy. You might need this." He heads out to his car as they all stand at the window waving goodbye. MC rushes off just as he did when leaving Beverly.

Ned looks on in disgust.

CHAPTER THIRTY THREE

Just like a few weeks earlier, a soft breeze brings slight movement to the orange leaves that barely cling to the maples up and down Carter Bend. The bronze statue of Vince Carter still sits proudly guarding the cul-de-sac at the end of the road.

The barber shop, gas station, ice cream shop, grocery store, library, and the coffee shack come into view. Friendly faces pass on the street.

Harper and Grump sit at their regular table. Something is different. The checker board is gone. It has been replaced with a candyland board. Still neither of them pays any attention to the game.

Grump shakes his head and blinks his eyes rapidly. He looks around the room noticing the chimes ring as Mort and Dangie enter.

"Mornin Dangie." Harper lifts his head for a moment and then looks back down at the candyland board shrugging his shoulders. "Am I red or black?"

Grump stares out the window.

Mort and Dangie stand speaking to Kamptin. They laugh.

Grump smiles and becomes anxious like when a dog sees his master after missing him for a few days. Harper leans over to look out the window with him. He also becomes excited.

The chimes ring again and Harper smiles. "Hey Gladstone, would you mind?"

ferf ziamond

He holds his coffee cup up to let MC know he needs a refill. Grump follows suit.

"Sure thing Harper, Grump." MC puts his bags down as Mort and Dangie make their way over to greet him. They exchange hugs in complete excitement.

Once they settle down Kamptin places three cups of coffee and a package of crackers on the counter. "These are on the house."

"Thanks Kamptin. How've you been?"

Kamptin gives a big smile and a thumbs up to MC.

MC, followed by Mort and Dangie, brings the coffees to Harper and Grump. He places them down on their table. "Hey candyland. Can I play the winner?"

Mort laughs. "There are no winners at this table." Dangie slaps Mort and they hug gently. MC becomes confused.

Mort looks at MC while in the middle of the hug. "I told you I had big news. We're getting married. You're my best man!"

MC's coffee cup falls to the floor and spills. He stares at the two of them.

"Look. He's all choked up. I told you he'd be speechless." Mort waits for a word from MC.

"I hope he's not this speechless when he makes the toast at the wedding." Dangie looks concerned.

The chimes ring once again and MC stares at the door. His eyes follow a customer who enters.

"He's really in shock."

Exchanging Pleasantries

"MC are you okay?"

Still not a word from MC.

"Stop messing around. What's wrong?"

"Mort do something!"

MC continues to stare at the counter. His mouth and eyes go from lost to confusion to contempt to extreme happiness. He too looks like a dog rejoined with a loved one.

A voice calls over. "Need help cleaning that spill?" It is Dabni. She stands in front of the counter holding two coffee cups.

"Wh- wh- what are you doing here?" He takes a step toward her. She puts the cups down on the counter.

"I was taking a trip up to Maine with my dad. We just stopped for a cup."

"I thought I'd never see you again."

"I'm glad we chose this exit for gas."

"That's the nicest thing anyone's ever said to me." MC goes in for the hug.

"We can't lose touch ever again." Dabni squeezes him tight.

The chimes ring once again.

Mort and Dangie look at each other with some confusion. A small African American child stands next to Mort. It is Dream child.

Mort continues to stare at MC and Dabni. "Who is she and what is she doing here?"

Dangie shrugs. Dream child looks at Mort. "Hell if I know. I told her to get her ass in the kitchen."

ferf ziamond

"You must be MC's new tag along." Dangie puts out her hand. Dream child shakes it.

"He sure has his hands full once again."

"The name's Gladstone. I play football. One day I'll be on the New York Jets! Nice to meet you white folks." Dream child moves over and sits on Grumps lap. "Candyland! Can I play?"

Grump doesn't know if he should push him off or hold him tight. Something makes him hold on tight.

Mort whispers to Dangie. "That's the long lost grandson I told you about." Dangie has a look of shock.

MC has never looked as happy as he does at this moment. He holds on tight to Dabni, he notices Dream child. He is confused how his dream came to reality but he happily accepts it. "I got my girl. I got my new little brother. Now all I need is a job."

A sound that has never been heard before in the coffee shack is heard. Everyone's attention is on the bags that MC put down by the door. A closer look reveals his Boston Herald phone ringing.

CHAPTER THIRTY FOUR

The Marigold Café is dark, cold and lonely. The only one seen on the premises is Ned. He reads a review of his most recent story. It is the one he concocted of the notes he took whenever MC showed up at the Marigold. He slurps on a fratte latte.

"I am exceedingly depleted. The ramblings from page one to page twenty-one exasperated my every ounce of energy. Sound familiar? Your story about my experience is not going to make it. Reason being, you are missing all of the golden words offered by one Carter Bell. If you would have considered that, you may have had a best seller instead of living in a best cellar. You should also consider using the two words for meeting some girl in a gym, in a coffee shop, on a writer's website. Quick blurbs about your days, simple greetings. It's all work, chasing dreams, and exchanging pleasantries. The wealthiest of writers have no fortunes in money, although they live to share all they create. Yours Truly, THE MARIGOLD MOOCH." Anger fills Ned's face.

"You no good son of a bitch!" He continues reading another portion of the website. "Third prize goes to Sirens in the sky." He scrolls down. "Second prize goes to Blaring Siren." He continues to scroll. "First prize goes to A Day in the Life?" He is put out. "What? Where

ferf ziamond

is my prize? My story was the best! This site is fixed!" He begins to choke on his fratte latte just like Ann wished some time ago.

Monique walks out of her office. "Oh, you're still here?"

Ned tries to regain his composure. "Are you happy to see me? Or are you just exchanging pleasantries?"

IN CLOSING:

MC and Dabni stand in front of the Vince Carter statue holding hands. The plaque is visible.

Dedicated to Vince Carter.
A brave soul who built a place
for all of us to escape the wrath
of hatred and prejudice. May love
and freedom always reign in Beverly MA.
Or maybe a passerby can just remember
why this town was created.

THE END.

Exchanging Pleasantries

Screenplay

Written by
ferf ziamond

FADE IN

EXT. CARTER BEND - DAY

An intersection with a street sign reading CARTER BEND and TRENIS' DE BEVERLY DRIVE appears.

A breeze brings movement to the leaves and trees on the road.

A bronze statue of a man sits in the cul-de-sac at the end of the road. The name VINCE CARTER is engraved on the plaque.

A sign reads WELCOME TO TRENIS' VILLAGE. Beyond the sign a barber shop, gas station, ice cream shop, grocery store, library, and the coffee shack.

Friendly faces pass on the street in front of the run down coffee shack.

INT. COFFEE SHACK - DAY

Unkempt, historic in appearance, a few scattered customers, most of which are in their twenties.

Two men in their seventies sit at a table, a checkerboard between them.

The grizzled old men, HARPER and GRUMP. Harper sits gazing out of a dingy window. Grump stares at the checkerboard mesmerized.

Grump shakes his head. He looks around the room noticing the scattered customers.

> GRUMP
> Whose turn is it anyway?

> HARPER
> Hell if I know. My mind got lost out the winda.

The small window facing Ludlum Avenue, the third of the three village streets, has cob webs in the corners and crust scattered along the panes. Weeds grow outside obscuring most of the view. A young woman walks to the door.

A brown door chime rings as she enters. Harper lifts his head.

> HARPER (CONT.)
> Mornin Dangie.

Harper looks at the checkerboard shrugging his shoulders.

> HARPER (CONT.)
> Am I red or black?

DANGIE, mid twenties, brunette, cute, walks in unfolding dollar bills she pulls from her purse.

> DANGIE
> Hi ya Harper.

She looks to the large man in a tank top behind the counter. His hair and beard are a greasy mess.

>   DANGIE (CONT.)
>   The usual Kamptin.

She lays two dollars beside the old fashioned register, smiles.

>   KAMPTIN
>   Dangie.

Kamptin places her cup of coffee on the worn counter. She picks it up and walks past Harper and Grump's table.

>   DANGIE
>   Who's winning?

She looks at the checkerboard and takes a seat two tables back.

>   HARPER
>   I think I am.

Harper looks up as the chimes ring again.

>   HARPER (CONT.)
>   Oh, this character.

MORT, twenties, walks toward the counter. Kamptin shakes his hand. They speak then Mort heads toward Dangie, slows down by Grump.

>   MORT
>   Black winning?

                    GRUMP
  Black's always losing in my book.

Grump stares at Mort who takes a seat across from Dangie.

Mort looks at Dangie, eyes glowing.

                    MORT
  Hey Dangie.

                    DANGIE
  Good morning. Starting in already?

Mort lifts himself out of his chair a fraction peering at Grump.

                    MORT
  Candyland is friendlier!

He eases back down into the chair. Dangie lets out a giggle, covers her mouth.

Grump looks back at Mort for a moment before Harper interrupts.

                    HARPER
  Gladstone's on his way up the
  street. He can get us a refill.

                    GRUMP
  Thank you young man, you're very
  enlightening.

Grump turns his head back to Harper and whispers.

GRUMP (CONT.)
What the hell is candyland?

The chimes ring again, another young man enters and looks over. He has a bag over his shoulder with a logo on it. TRENIS' TIMES.

Harper holds his coffee cup up. Grump follows suit.

HARPER
Hey Gladstone, would you mind?

MC is his name but the guys call him Gladstone.

MC
Sure thing Harper, Grump.

MC looks back at Mort and Dangie.

MC (CONT.)
Hey Mort. I may have done it!

He holds up a piece of paper then looks back at Kamptin who places three cups and a package of crackers on the counter.

Mort puts on a face.

MORT
He may have done it once again. I may just pay a newspaper to hire him at this point.

                    DANGIE
            That's so mean. He tries hard. And
            he's so adorable.

Mort's straight face becomes a sarcastic grin.

                    MORT
            Your brother.

MC balances three coffee cups on his way to Harper and Grumps table.

                    MORT (CONT.)
            Maybe now we'll be able to get his
            cell phone number. Better yet, now
            maybe he'll stop talking about
            that website he puts his stories
            on.

MC stops by Harper and Grump. Harper hands MC a dollar.

                    HARPER
            Keep the change Gladstone.

                    MC
            Thanks Harper.

He slips the bill in his pocket and sits next to Mort.

                    MC (CONT.)
            I'm out of here guys.

                    DANGIE
            What do you mean?

                    MC
            I got a call. It's time to move on.

MORT
On your Boston Herald phone?

MC
This is the big time. New York Newsday.

DANGIE
Are you serious?

MORT
You're really gonna go down there? What's wrong with your Trenis' Times gig?

MC
Give me a break. The biggest pay I ever got for writing for them was this bag.

He holds the bag up. Grump turns around.

GRUMP
Them black kids'll eat you alive. You don't stand a chance.

He turns back around.

Dangie, MC and Mort laugh. Mort shakes his head.

MORT
What is wrong with that idiot?

DANGIE
You'd be a grump too if your daughter in-law ran off with your grandson.

                    MC
          Even worse, not ever meeting that
          daughter in-law or grandson.

                    MORT
          Better for the daughter in-law and
          grandson. They don't need to know
          this grouch of a granddad.

Mort laughs slightly.

                    MORT (CONT.)
          I met the grandson once. It's no
          wonder Grump's son kept a lid on
          that whole part of his life. Grump
          never would have approved. I could
          never forget that kid.

                    MC
          C'mon, he's just an old man. He
          doesn't realize half of what he
          says. Do you think I should worry
          about the black kids?

                    DANGIE
          I can't believe you're actually
          considering leaving us. What are
          you going to do with Ferf?

                    MC
          He's coming with me.

                    DANGIE
          That's a long ride. It might not be
          good for her.

                    MC
          He'll be fine.

DANGIE
She wasn't so great last time she was in a car.

MORT
Five years and neither of you know the sex of that damn cat.

He shakes his head.

At the same time Dangie and MC state their beliefs.

DANGIE
She's a girl!

MC
He's a boy!

MORT
Exactly!

Triumphant, to concern.

MORT (CONT.)
So, you're really gonna do this?

MC
I don't have a choice.

Grump chimes in again.

GRUMP
Remember what I said when you're laying on the ground somewhere looking up at some black kid begging for your life.

EXT. COFFEE SHACK

From the window the group continues their conversation.

EXT. NEW YORK CITY

Light rainfall glides against the tall buildings. The streets are filled with yellow taxis at red lights.

Pedestrians with umbrellas are on every corner. The honking of car horns is heard. This is lower Manhattan.

Between two fifty story buildings and off to the side, a big gold and black store sign sticks out. MARIGOLD CAFÉ.

INT. MARIGOLD CAFÉ

The inside of the café is a tremendous step up compared to the coffee shack. The door alone is made from the finest materials. Walls and floors of marble, ceiling fans, chandeliers, each modernized table and chair set complete with its own internet connection.

Off to the side is a large shelf of exotic cookies.

Patrons set up scattered offices sipping from coffee mugs.

One customer stands out above the rest. NED. Tall, thin, mid-thirties, short blonde hair. He takes up two tables. Laptop, latte, and newspaper on one. Briefcase, cell phone, beeper, scattered folders, and pages of notes on the other.

He takes his eyes away from the laptop as a waitress passes by. Her name tag reads ANN.

Ned holds up his cup.

          NED
Another Fratte latte Ginger.

She has a perturbed look.

          ANN
Ginger hasn't worked here in months.

She walks to the counter and whispers to another waitress.

          ANN (CONT.)
He's such an asshole.

The other waitress, cute and quiet, DABNI. She laughs and hands Ann a cup.

          DABNI
One fratte latte.

          ANN
I hope he chokes on it.

          DABNI.
You're too much.

                    ANN
            His arrogance is too much.

Ann brings the cup to him as a phone rings behind the counter.

                ANN (CONT.)
            You got that Dabni?

Dabni picks up the phone.

                    DABNI
            Daddy I miss you! How are things
            at home?

INT. KITCHEN

In a small town outside of Boston, her dad, early fifties, a short, well groomed, pleasant man sits in a cozy, brown and white, neatly furnished kitchen.

Scattered pictures held by magnet ornaments fill the refrigerator door. Dabni can be seen in a couple of the photos. A sign on an ornamental chef reads, "No bitchin in Ginny's kitchen."

On a windowsill sits a small birdhouse with a fake parakeet sitting on a perch.

Her dad has an enormous smile.

INTERCUT

>   DAD
> Come on home baby. I can set you
> up with your own place if you're
> ready.
>
>   DABNI
> You know I'd love that daddy, but
> this just isn't the time. Besides,
> when it is time, I'll be setting
> myself up.
>
>   DAD
> I know you will honey.

Some rattling is overheard in the background.

>   DAD (CONT.)
> Oh wait baby.
>
>   DABNI
> Daddy?

She becomes concerned.

>   DABNI (CONT.)
> Is everything okay?
>
>   DAD
> I have to go for now baby.

He is distracted.

>   DAD (CONT.)
> You're mother just spilled some
> coffee on herself. I have to clean
> her up.

                    DABNI
          Is she all right?

                    DAD
          I'll give you a call later.

                    DABNI
          Dad?

                    DAD
          She'll be fine sweetheart.

Ann looks to Dabni as she puts the phone down.

                    ANN
          Is everything all right?

                    DABNI
          It always comes down to coffee in
          my life.

They both have a relieved look.

EXT. COFFEE SHACK - DAY

Dangie and MC stand facing one another. Dangie's dungaree jacket is two sizes too big. MC's hooded sweat jacket is rather snug. The wind messes their hair slightly.

                    DANGIE
          How are you going to break it to
          little Francis that you're leaving?
          He'll be crushed.

MC looks at her.

                    MC
Oh c'mon. Little Francis? How long
has it been? Little Francis is not
little anymore and I haven't done
Tag Along since he turned sixteen.

                 DANGIE
I guess.

                    MC
Why are you reaching for this
stuff? It's not making my situation
any easier.

                 DANGIE
Having a brother like you don't
make my life any easier either. I
have a situation too you know.

                    MC
What situation is that?

                 DANGIE
I could have a situation.

                    MC
Can you get on with it? I'm tired
of the word situation already. And
stop calling me your brother!

                 DANGIE
You might as well be.

                    MC
Why is that?

                    DANGIE
          What other reason could you have
          for not sleeping with me?

                      MC
          Don't do this to me again Dangie.

He tries to change the subject.

                   MC (CONT.)
          How'd you get such a silly name
          anyway? Dangie?

                    DANGIE
          You're the bozo that gave me
          that name. My name is Angie, not
          Dangie.

                      MC
          Oh yea.

MC walks down the sidewalk. Dangie follows.

                   MC (CONT.)
          Look, it's not gonna be forever.
          And it's not even that far.

                    DANGIE
          Can I visit you?

                      MC
          Let's not push it.

                    DANGIE
          I always wanted to see New York.

                    MC
          I probably won't have room for
          guests.

                  DANGIE
          New York. The city that never
          sleeps.

                    MC
          Sleeping arrangements might be
          tough.

                  DANGIE
          They say it's the greatest city in
          the world.

                    MC
          I'll give you a call after I settle
          in.

Dangie pulls a photo out of her purse.

                  DANGIE
          At least hold onto this.

It is a picture of Dangie sitting on a large rock in front of a lake.

               DANGIE (CONT.)
          Look at it when you miss me.

A clanging sound comes from up the block. They look at each other.

                    MC
          The Angel of lost parts.

                    DANGIE
    The Angel of lost parts.

An old blue Buick comes creeping down the street backfiring. A closer look reveals two different color blue paints, bald tires, no side view mirrors, scuff marks, a missing head lamp, and a dangling license plate.

Behind the steering wheel sits a proud Mort. He rolls down the window with great difficulty.

                    MORT
    She's still breathin.

MC coughs and waves his hand.

                    MC
    Breathin with emphysema.

                    MORT
    What do you say, one last ride for the city boy before his departure?

MC and Dangie climb in. Smoke blows from the tail pipe.

EXT. MANHATTAN STREET – DAY

Smoke flows from a manhole on the avenue. A constant stream of yellow cabs drive through the cloud and continue to the next traffic light. A policeman waves the automobiles on.

Crowds form on the corners waiting to cross. Three white boys' ages twelve to thirteen run between the cars. The policeman hollers.

The boys laugh, continue running. The smallest of the three, CLETTA, turns around to give the officer the finger. The officer steps forward, hesitates, steps back.

Cletta turns around, hurries along, slams into a large woman in a flowery dress. He hits the floor as the other two boys pause to laugh.

The woman clenches her pocket book. She notices the laughter, swings the pocket book at Cletta, misses. Her belongings fly out of the bag.

Embarrassed, she bends down to pick up the items. The boys continue running. The police officer grins.

The boys stop in front of the Marigold Café.

One of the boys looks to Cletta

          BOY ONE
Whatta ya say Cletta, steal a drink to get refreshed?

          CLETTA
Let's check it out.

The other boys look up to Cletta.

INT. MARIGOLD CAFÉ

They enter. The customers become quiet. Ned continues to type away. He takes up two tables, his belongings sprawled around. He's in mid conversation on his cell phone.

NED
Oh yes. I just finished crushing another dream. Wait till this amateur reads my review of his rubbish.

He continues to type.

NED (CONT.)
What's another word for extremely bored?

He waits as Cletta stands nearby at the cookie display.

NED (CONT.)
That's it!

Ned hollers.

NED (CONT.)
I am exceedingly depleted, the ramblings from page one to page twenty-one exasperated my every ounce of energy.

Cletta pockets a package of cookies without anyone noticing. He walks to the refrigerator where the other boys stand.

A beautiful young woman in her early thirties, MONIQUE the shop manager, approaches.

> MONIQUE
> Can I give you any assistance gentlemen?

Cletta grips the cookies in his pocket.

> CLETTA
> You sure can.

He is obviously smitten.

> MONIQUE
> Okay little man, you can take it back out on the street now.

She is polite and displeased.

Cletta makes his way toward the exit, the other two follow.

> CLETTA
> Could you show us your boobs first?

Cletta walks faster. Most of the patrons look on in disgust. A random coffee drinker lets out a chuckle.

> MONIQUE
> That's enough. Keep walking.

She walks behind them. They make their way back to the sidewalk. The door shuts.

Frustrated and slightly amused, Monique walks toward Dabni at the counter.

>   DABNI
> You handled that well.

>   MONIQUE
> Not as well as I would have liked to.

>   DABNI
> I guess you have to cut some slack to children these days.

>   MONIQUE
> I'd like to cut more than slack on that little wise ass.

EXT. MC's HOUSE - EVENING

Mort's Angel of lost parts sits smoking and sputtering even though the car is turned off. MC's red Mazda is close by in front. It is filled with bags and boxes.

MC places a final box in the back seat, Mort and Dangie look on.

>   MC
> Well, I guess this is so long for now.

MC looks inside the pet carrier on the passenger seat. The eyes of his grayish, black Ocicat, Ferf, from the darkness.

Dangie pulls MC to her and holds onto him.

                DANGIE
You take care of yourself. Call us. Even if it means using your Boston Herald phone.

She takes a step back. Mort shakes his hand.

                MORT
Later man.

MC pulls him in closer.

                MC
It's been a load of laughs.

He walks around the car to the driver's side.

He pulls away, his hand sticks out of the window waving. His mom and dad are at the front window with their arms around each other. Mort looks to them, smiles, and then back at Dangie.

The red Mazda gets further down the road and disappears. Dangie and Mort stare at one another.

The red Mazda makes its way onto the highway.

INT. MC'S CAR

Music plays softly, MC talks to himself.

> MC
> I had to tell them I was called. It's the only way I could have left with any pride.

He grips the steering wheel.

> MC (CONT.)
> So what if I'm not really working for Newsday? So what if I told everyone my dream of writing is coming true? So what if that dream has become a fairy tale?

He taps the steering wheel and nods his head to the music.

> MC (CONT.)
> Besides, they're offering me something no one in their right mind could turn down. A raise, a months paid rent in an upscale apartment complex, and a chance to experience city life.

He glances out the passenger side window at the cows.

> MC (CONT.)
> Mooooooooo!

He chuckles. Ferf is becoming restless.

                    MC (CONT.)
          You like that Ferf?

He taps the pet carrier.

                    MC (CONT.)
          Maybe New York is the place to
          discover whatever it is that I
          need to discover.

Ferf becomes louder and louder.

                    MC (CONT.)
          Come on Ferf. We still have a long
          ride ahead.

He raises the radio volume.

Outside pastures, horse ranches, farms, and an occasional house.

                    MC (CONT.)
          This is my chance to lie about
          my life in a positive way. Maybe
          Newsday will give me a shot.

He sings along with the music while Ferf sounds like he is being tortured.

EXT. MC's CAR - NIGHT

Darkness falls. The white lines on the highway are all that is visible under moon light. Ferf's cries are loud.

INT. MARIGOLD CAFÉ - MORNING

As the sun rises Monique opens. A heavy set African American woman is the first customer. She makes her way to a table as MC'S car pulls up outside.

Monique brings the woman a cup of coffee as MC walks to the entrance.

              MONIQUE
Here you go Maisy. Careful. It's hot.

              MAISY
Thanks Mo.

Maisy opens her newspaper.

              MAISY (CONT.)
I may need your umbrella again hun. It looks like the clouds are coming back.

              MONIQUE
No problem.

Dabni straightens out the counter and runs around making sure all of the coffee pots are set up correctly. The sounds of brewing coffee and the smell of twenty flavors combined smacks MC in the face as he walks through the door.

Monique grabs a newspaper and heads to her office. She winks at Dabni.

> MONIQUE (CONT.)
> Go easy on him. He looks like an out of towner.

Dabni smiles as Monique enters her office.

> DABNI
> Good morning. Welcome to the Marigold Café. May I help you?

She gives MC a big smile.

MC continues to stare at the office door.

> MC
> Uh, yea, I think so.

He seems dumbfounded.

> MC (CONT.)
> Regular, cream and sugar.

Dabni seems a little confused.

> DABNI
> Sure, what flavor?

> MC
> Flavor? Coffee. You said this is a café, right?

> DABNI
> I know coffee but what kind? We have lattes, coolatas, Mocha chinos, cremalinas, frappaccinos, creamy dippen frattas.

                    MC
          I don't understand. What is all of
          that?

Dabni tilts her head to the side and
smiles. She has a cute look.

                    DABNI
          Monique said you were an out of
          towner.

MC's face lights up.

                    MC
          Who's Monique? The woman that went
          in the back?

                    DABNI
          That's the manager, Monique. The
          thirty one year old princess of
          the East side.

She looks to the office door and then
back at MC.

                    DABNI (CONT.)
          So out of towner, where you from?

She pours a cup for him.

MC continues to stare at the office door.

                    MC
          You probably never heard of it.
          Beverly Massachusetts. Up north.
          We have regular coffee up in those
          parts.

She hands him the smoking cup.

                    DABNI
          This is as regular as we get here.
          Lemme know if it needs more cream
          or sugar.

He takes a small sip.

                     MC
          It's good.

He blows on the cup.

                 MC (CONT.)
          Different, but good.

                    DABNI
          So, what do you do in Beverly
          Massachusetts?

                     MC
          That's what brought me to New York.
          My company has an office way up
          north that is downsizing. They
          offered me an incredible deal to
          come down here. I had to take it.

                    DABNI
          I guess you're very valuable to
          the company.

                     MC
          I don't know if I'd say that.

Dabni speaks with a convincing tone.

                    DABNI
          They seem to have wanted to keep
          you.

At first MC has a happy, proud look. Then it changes.

                    MC
    Unless it was a mistake.

                    DABNI
    I have family near Boston. They
    call to scare me sometimes. My mom
    can't seem to hold a coffee cup
    like she used to.

She catches herself.

                    DABNI (CONT.)
    Sorry, sometimes I just keep
    yapping if no one stops me.

                    MC
    I like it. You're a good yapper.

                    DABNI
    Sometimes when I miss her I'll
    send some refrigerator magnets or
    kitchen ornaments. See? There I go
    again. So how far is Beverly from
    Boston? My dad and I probably pass
    it on our trips to Maine.

His eyes bulge a bit.

                    MC
    It's quite a hike north of Boston.

He has a look of achievement.

                    MC (CONT.)
    I know Boston though. I'm trying
    to get a job at the Herald.

132

                    DABNI
          Photographer?

                     MC
          Writer.

He grins.

                 MC (CONT.)
          Well, part time, hoping to become
          a writer.

                    DABNI
          Oh, you should meet.

She pauses.

                DABNI (CONT.)
          Oh never mind.

                     MC
          Meet who?

                    DABNI
          I just thought of a guy Ned
          that spends his life here. He's
          a writer, but the girls seem to
          dislike him.

She makes a face.

                     MC
          You just reminded me of a friend
          of mine, Dangie.

                    DABNI
          How funny, my name is Dabni.

                    MC
Isn't that something?

He looks back at the office door.

                 MC (CONT.)
Well, her name is actually Angie.
I just called her damn Angie so
many times that Dangie became her
name.

                   DABNI
That's funny.

The office door suddenly opens a crack.

                  MONIQUE
Ann here yet Dabni?

Dabni looks out the window. On the corner, Ann waiting for the light.

                   DABNI
She's right across the street.

                  MONIQUE
The rush should be beginning soon.

Monique sticks her head out. MC looks frozen. After a moment he waves.

                    MC
Uh.

Monique gives a wiggling finger wave to him.

MONIQUE
How ya doing doll?

She steps back into the office as MC continues to stare. A few customers make their way in. Ann follows them.

DABNI
Good morning Ann. Monique was asking for you.

ANN
I'm five minutes late again.

DABNI
By the way, this is.

Dabni looks over at MC who can't keep his eyes off of the office door.

DABNI (CONT.)
I'm sorry. I didn't get your name.

He comes out of his trance, looks back at Dabni.

MC
Sorry? Monique?

DABNI
Your name.

MC
I'm sorry. It's MC.

He smiles at Ann who puts on an apron.

Dabni counts out some singles from the register.

             DABNI
   So, whatta you do for fun up
   north?

             MC
   Funny but we spent most our time
   around a coffee place up there
   too.

He laughs slightly.

             MC (CONT.)
   The shack it's called.

Dabni smiles at him while in the middle of counting, her lips moving.

             DABNI
   Oh yea?

MC leans on the counter.

             MC
   Not as fancy as your place. Or
   should I say Monique's place?

He can't help but smile when saying her name.

             MC (CONT.)
   I used to belong to an
   organization called Tag Along.

             DABNI
   What's that?

                    MC
I would act like a big brother or
older cousin to a kid. His name is
Francis.

                  DABNI
Like Big Brother.

                   MC
That's what I said.

                  DABNI
You said like a, big brother. Not
Big Brother.

                   MC
What's your point?

                  DABNI
There is an organization down
here called Big Brother. You help
nurture kids who don't have any
family.

                   MC
That's what Tag Along is.

                  DABNI
Glad we established that.

She lets out a small laugh.

              DABNI (CONT.)
I belong to Big Sister.

                   MC
I guess that's the girl's version.

He's obviously being cute.

> DABNI
> Funny. You should look into it down here.

> MC
> I would, but what if they give me a black kid?

He has fear in his eyes. Maisy cannot take her eyes off of MC. Her mouth is wide open. Nothing comes out.

> DABNI
> Excuse me?

MC is nervous and embarrassed.

> MC
> I gotta check on my cat.

He walks to the door, everyone watches him leave.

He holds the door for Ned who enters.

INT. APARTMENT BUILDING - DAY

MC walks through a revolving door into a lavish and luxurious New York City apartment building. With pet carrier in hand, his eyes bulge and take in all of the sights the lobby has to offer. Chandeliers, bell boys, gold luggage carriers, a four story ceiling with two stairways circling an elevator. It is a long walk from the door to the front desk. A pretty blonde WOMAN with half a smile greets him at the desk.

>   WOMAN
> May I help you?

MC puts the pet carrier down. Ferf is still loud and disturbing.

>   MC
> Shhhhh. We'll be home in a minute.

He pulls out his work ID and apartment paperwork.

>   MC (CONT.)
> Yes ma'am. My job made
> arrangements for me here.

As the woman snickers and hands the papers back to him she puts two fingers over her mouth.

>   WOMAN
> This is not where they made the
> arrangements. I'm sorry.

>   MC
> No?

>   WOMAN
> What you want to do is go two
> blocks south.

She points. MC studies her eyes.

                    WOMAN (CONT.)
    Make a left, and it is on the next
    corner. It's the Brolstar, not the
    Borellis.

MC takes the papers back.

                    MC
    Sorry. My mistake.

He makes his way out of the Borellis.
She calls after him.

                    WOMAN
    Have a nice evening.

He waves a hand up while approaching
the revolving doors.

EXT. STREET

Out on the street MC zips his jacket up.
His car is parked next to a homeless
shelter.

                    MC
    I better leave the car there.
    I'm not searching for a spot for
    another hour and a half.

Annoyed, he walks the two blocks south.
At the next corner a HOMELESS MAN
stops him with his hand out. The man
wears rags. He can barely complete a
sentence.

                    HOMELESS MAN
> Pom a dollar. Pom a quarter. Bar
> since. Car a home.

MC places Ferf's carrier on the ground and pulls a few bills out of his pocket.

                         MC
> I'd like to give you two dollars
> but I only have a single and a
> couple of fives. I don't suppose
> you have any change?

The man stares at MC. MC stares back for a moment. He looks down at the money. He hands over a five.

                    HOMELESS MAN
> Mmmm, non pel. Dank you.

The man makes some noises and MC hurries off. He finds himself under an awning that reads, THE BROLSTAR.

INT. APARTMENT - LATER

MC sits on a large bed staring at Ferf who is finally out of his carrier.

                         MC
> It was a rough ride boy.

He takes a closer look at the cat.

                    MC (CONT.)
> Girl. Whatever you are.

Ferf jumps off the bed. The three room apartment appears to be more than the two of them need. Fine oak furniture, a large ceiling fan, modernized kitchen, and a balcony.

>   MC (CONT.)
>   I won't take you in the car ever
>   again. I promise.

MC falls back on the bed. His hands cover his eyes and slowly move down to his mouth and chin.

>   MC (CONT.)
>   I can't believe how stupid I was
>   at that café. What a fool I am.
>   How could I talk down about black
>   people when I never really got to
>   know one of them? It's all that
>   idiot Grumps fault.

He points the remote control at the television.

>   MC (CONT.)
>   Football. Maybe I should join
>   that Big Brother thing. I could
>   start fresh with another kid like
>   Francis. We could throw a football
>   around.

He turns to the side.

>   MC (CONT.)
>   Big Brother organization.

EXT. STREET - DAY

DREAM SEQUENCE

There is a *SWOOSH*, as if a ball is being sucked through a vacuum chute. The *swoosh* is followed by a TWELVE YEAR OLD AFRICAN AMERICAN BOY'S voice.

                    DREAM CHILD
          Not what you were expecting?

MC and a child stand side by side. Only their heads turn to speak to one another, they never make eye contact. MC is taken aback by the boy's appearance.

                         MC
          You're the one assigned to me?

They appear to be walking down the middle of a busy New York street, almost gliding. A restaurant called QUERO GLEANO, other store fronts, moving vehicles, and other pedestrians drift past them. The only sound is their two voices until the homeless man appears on a corner counting five dollar bills and making noises.

                    HOMELESS MAN
          Mmmm, non pel. Dank you. Pom a
          dollar. Pom a quarter. Bar since.
          Car a home.

MC looks down toward the Dream child.

                    MC
          No, not exactly what I was
          expecting.

                    DREAM CHILD
          Cause I'm black!

                    MC
          You are black.

                    DREAM CHILD
          It's African American asshole!

                    MC
          I apologize.

                    DREAM CHILD
          You think we coloreds are good at
          football. That's all we're good for
          right?

       Dream child becomes angry.

                    DREAM CHILD (CONT.)
          Well you can blow it out your fat
          white.

       MC is awakened by a referee's whistle
       on the television.

                    MC
          Damn that Grump.

       MC rolls over again.

INT. COFFEE SHACK - DAY

       Kamptin walks away from Harper and
       Grumps table after bringing them two

cups of coffee. They are in the middle of a game of checkers. Harper stares out the window.

                    HARPER
    Thank you.

The door chimes ring as Mort and Dangie walk in together. Mort laughs. Dangie looks at the newspaper.

                    MORT
    He would have liked that. Writers
    wanted.

Dangie folds the newspaper and rests it under her arm.

Harper takes his attention away from the window and watches the two of them speaking to Kamptin who hands them each a cup of coffee. Mort pays and they walk towards Harper and Grump. Dangie smiles at them.

                    DANGIE
    Who's winning?

                    HARPER
    I probably am. I can't even tell
    if he's awake.

Harper nods in Grump's direction.

Mort looks at Grump.

                    MORT
    He's smarter when he's sleeping.

                    HARPER
          Where's Gladstone? Not traveling
          in your circles anymore?

                     MORT
          He's a big city boy now. Remember?
          He took off for New York.

Harper thinks for a moment.

                    HARPER
          That's right.

Grumps eyes open, he looks at Mort.

                     GRUMP
          Them black kids eat him up yet?

Mort adds some sarcasm.

                     MORT
          He lives!

                    DANGIE
          We haven't spoken to him since
          he left, but I'm sure no one has
          given him a hard time.

Grump laughs lightly. He becomes insistent.

                     GRUMP
          Give it a little time. Them black
          kids'll get him.

Mort sits down at the table two back. Dangie follows after smiling at the men. She takes the seat directly across from Mort, looks deep into his eyes.

INT. SUBWAY CAR - DAWN

MC sits on the subway. He has on a suit, tie, and sneakers.

There are only two others in the car. One, a BUSINESS MAN in a suit, he wears a pair of dress shoes. The second, an older woman, close to Harper and Grump in age. She is dressed in rags like the homeless man. She has a pushcart in front of her.

MC chooses the BUSINESS MAN to speak to.

>   MC
> This thing going near Wall Street?

The man lifts his eyes over his newspaper. After a moment he mumbles.

>   BUSINESS MAN
> Ten more stops or so.

>   MC
> Thanks.

>   BUSINESS MAN
> Uh huh.

>   MC
> Not as friendly as up north.

At the next stop, the express pulls up beside them. The business man jumps up quickly. He exits MC's train and hurries for the one across the platform. The older woman also gets off at the same stop. She makes her way down a stairway. MC is alone.

Two young African American teenage boys, KARU'L and JAMES get on the train and look at MC. KARU'L mumbles to JAMES.

                    KARU'L
        Boy must be lost or something.

They both laugh loudly and JAMES opens the sliding door leading to the next car. They exit.

MC becomes relieved.

                    MC
        Maybe I should have taken Grump
        more seriously. These black kids
        may want to kill me.

He stares at the sliding door as it opens again.

In walks Cletta and his two buddies. The three of them stop in front of MC and stare him down. He is nervous.

Cletta slaps one of his friends in the chest.

                    CLETTA
        What's this clown doing in our
        car?

One of the boys grabs MC by the shirt and pulls him up. MC makes two fists. Before he can use them the other kid rushes into him and knocks MC'S head against the door causing him to fall down. He is out cold.

The three kids become scared. They aren't sure what to do.

One of them kneels down and fumbles through MC's pockets, grabs his wallet. Cletta decides it is time to get away from the scene.

>   CLETTA (CONT.)
>   Drop that and let's move.

He heads to the sliding door as the others follow. The wallet is tossed next to MC. The cash is gone.

INT. APARTMENT - DAY

MC lies in the same position as in the subway car. This time he is on a worn dark green carpet next to a tan sofa equally tattered. A coffee table is off to the side. It seems to have the same appearance as the wood from the coffee shack. MC's eyes begin to blink open and shut. From a blur, two faces come into focus. They are Karu'l and James.

MC's face is pale and overcome with fear. He yells loudly begging for his life just as Grump said he would.

                    MC
    No please! Don't kill me! Please!

An older African American man, CARTER BELL, comes running in from another room. He stops and stares down at MC. After a moments pause he looks to Karu'l and James.

                  CARTER
    I told you boys he ain't dead.

Carter laughs and puts his hand out to help MC to his feet. While still holding his hand, he introduces himself.

              CARTER (CONT.)
    Carter Bell. Welcome to our home.

His smile is warm and hospitable.

              CARTER (CONT.)
    These my boys. Karu'l and James.

MC trembles when the young men extend their hands.

                    MC
    You ain't gonna kill me, right?

Carter puts his hands on his hips. He smiles.

                  CARTER
    Why would we kill you boy?

MC looks at the man with fear. He stutters for a moment.

                    MC
     J-just something an old man from
     back home said.

He stops himself.

                  CARTER
     Where you from boy?

                    MC
     Beverley Massachusetts sir.

                  CARTER
     They still got prejudice up there?
     That's not supposed to be.

                    MC
     I guess you can say that. They are
     two harmless old men though.

Carter takes a seat on the sofa. He
extends his hand for MC to take the
seat next to him.

                  CARTER
     Have a drink son?

MC is surprised.

                    MC
     Who me?

                  CARTER
     Karu'l lemme have a gin.

Carter waves his son into the
kitchen.

CARTER (CONT.)
Yes you.

MC
I guess I'll have a glass of water.

CARTER
Karu'l, make that two gins.

He turns back to MC.

CARTER (CONT.)
I know what happened.

Carter appears friendly. He places his hand on top of MC's.

CARTER (CONT.)
Some old fool told you that the colored folk will get ya. Let me tell you something. It ain't the colored folk that'll get ya, hell, it ain't the white folk that'll get ya either. It's not the Chinese, the Arab, the Muslim, the Jew folk. It's the rotten folk and the rotton folk only that'll get ya. And them folk come in all flavors. You gotta be wise enough to see under the wrapper boy.

MC stares mesmerized. Karu'l sets two glasses of gin down on the ragged coffee table and leaves the room with his brother.

Carter looks at MC.

CARTER (CONT.)
You got some place to be boy?

MC continues to stare.

MC
Carter? That's the same name as Carter Bend. Vince Carter.

The words just fall out of his mouth without any explanation.

CARTER
What you know about Vince Carter?

MC
Just that they named a road and a statue after him.

CARTER
I figured as much. Vince Carter built something. Built something amazing. As years pass, amazing turns into forgetfulness. My daddy didn't forget. He named me Carter for a reason.

MC returns to Carter's previous question.

MC
I guess I should be getting to work.

CARTER
Where's that?

INT. OFFICE BUILDING - DAY

MC sits in an office cubicle. The walls are a bluish grey. A black computer, matching phone, calculator, and pencil tin sit atop his metallic shined desk. He pulls a small calendar off the wall and proceeds to cross off the first day of September with a slash mark. He writes across the boxes of the last two weeks in big letters. FIND AN APARTMENT.

A large man in a suit, MR. GOHNZ stands over him.

MR. GOHNZ
Not a big deal that you're late. I'm surprised you made it at all.

Mr. Gohnz shakes his head while letting out a short cackle. He has somewhat of a box head with short hair and glasses.

MC taps his pen on the computer unit.

MC
What would you like me to begin with Mr. Gohnz?

Mr. Gohnz steps back.

MR. GOHNZ
We're just going to give you some space to get yourself settled today.

He continues to walk off.

                    MR. GOHNZ (CONT.)
          Call me if you need me.

He takes another four or five steps before
an attractive young woman hurries over
to him flapping pages in his face.

MC leans back.

                         MC
          Wow, another one.

He is impressed. He picks up his phone
and dials. At the same time he logs
onto his favorite website.

MC's eyes raise as the phone stops ringing.

                    MC (CONT.)
          Hey Mort!

INT. MORT'S APARTMENT - DAY

INTERCUT

Mort sits in his sloppy apartment at a
desk on the phone. His sneaker covered
feet are up on the desk. A photo of
Mort, MC, and Dangie as children on
a night stand. Clothes draped over
chairs and an exercise machine. A pizza
box lies on his bed. Sun shines through
his window, the shade sits raveled on
a dresser.

                         MORT
          MC? Ho-ly cow!

Excitement is in his voice.

                    MORT (CONT.)
           How is the big city boy?

MC sits swinging his swivel chair back and forth.

                    MC
           I don't know where to begin. So
           much happened on my first day. Let
           me just say that the ladies are
           incredible.

                    MORT
           It makes me real happy to hear you
           say that.

Mort has a tremendous grin.

                    MORT (CONT.)
           In love again?

                    MC
           This one girl at the coffee shop, she
           is the most beautiful woman I've ever
           seen.

                    MORT
           Every woman is the most beautiful
           woman you've ever seen.

                    MC
           The one that served me wasn't. She
           was cute, but she was no Monique.

                    MORT
           Monique?

MC

The manager. She's thirty one, has an apartment on the East side, she likes.

MORT

Oh, yea, you're not in love again.

MC

I also had a mishap on the subway.

MORT

Did Grump put a jinx on you?

MC is distracted by what he reads on his computer.

MC

You son of a.

MORT

What?

MC changes the subject.

MC

Remember that website I entered some of my writing on?

Mort comes off with a bit of a sarcastic tone.

MORT

How could I forget?

MC has a look of disappointment.

MC

Oh yea, you rather not discuss my writing.

Mort leans his head back and then pretends to care.

MORT

You know I'm just kidding. What happened on the website?

MC reads quickly to himself. He'd rather not share his sad news.

MC

It's nothing. Don't worry about it. Just seems like some guy wasn't so impressed by one of my short stories.

Mort feels he has to pretend a bit more.

MORT

Oh c'mon, I'm sorry. What'd the asshole say?

Mort's doorbell buzzes.

MORT (CONT.)

Oh shoot. Who could that be?

MC

The door?

MORT

I wasn't expecting anyone.

He takes his feet off the desk.

                    MC
　Go get it. I have work to get to
　anyway.

                    MORT
　Really? Okay man. Take it easy.

Mort quickly hangs up and walks to the
door. Dangie stands there as cute as
can be. They both soak each other in
for a moment.

INT. MC'S CUBICLE - DAY

　MC stares at his computer screen
　whispering a paragraph.

                    MC
　I am exceedingly depleted. The
　ramblings from page one to page
　twenty-one exasperated my every
　ounce of energy. The catastrophic
　disarray entitled "Sirens in
　the sky" is nothing short of a
　jumble of muddled unintelligible
　situations rolled into a major
　disaster.

A tear falls from MC's cheek. He quickly
signs off the computer, his hands shake.
He musters up a trifle of energy to get
from his desk to the men's room.

INT. MORT'S APARTMENT - DAY

Dangie sits at Mort's desk, Mort rubs her shoulders. Her eyes are shut, her smile beams.

Mort hesitates, then speaks.

MORT
That was MC on the phone.

Dangie opens her eyes, looks excited, pauses, and then acts cool.

DANGIE
How is he doing?

MORT
He got some feedback on his writing.

DANGIE
How was it?

MORT
Not sure. That's when you came in.

DANGIE
How did he sound?

MORT
He's not gonna make it down there.

Dangie seems concerned and protective.

DANGIE
Aw, that's mean.

                    MORT
    Whatta ya still have a thing for
    him?

Dangie changes the subject.

                    DANGIE
    Let's get a cup at the shack.

Mort throws his denim jacket over her
shoulders.

                    MORT
    Sure.

EXT. MARIGOLD CAFÉ

MC stands in front of the café peeping
through the window.

Inside Dabni organizes coffee pots and
pastries.

                    MC
    No Maisy. I guess it's safe to go
    in.

He walks in.

INT. MARIGOLD CAFÉ

Dabni takes one look at him. She is
not pleased.

                    DABNI
    Oh you.

MC approaches her.

MC

Please let me explain.

Dabni walks from the counter to a table. She sprays it and wipes it with some paper towels.

DABNI

Explain that you are a racist?

MC steps closer and puts his hand on the spray bottle.

MC

Maybe it looked like that. It's just that someone from up north drilled some negative thoughts about certain people in my head before I came down here.

He holds the spray bottle. Dabni lets go. She looks into his eyes.

DABNI

Up north huh?

MC

Your home town too.

DABNI

It's beautiful, but some people are set in their ways. I know how that can be.

MC has a look of relief.

MC

So, this Big Brother organization. Where can I find it?

Dabni pulls out her pad and pen. They sit.

                    DABNI
    It's simple.

She begins to write as the door opens. Maisy walks in.

                    MAISY
    Hi Dabni.

She takes a closer look at the two of them.

                MAISY (CONT.)
    Oh, it's Mr. Klux of the Klan.

MC quickly stands up.

                    MC
    Maisy. I'm awfully sorry. See, I'm new in town and.

She cuts him off.

                    MAISY
    Save it Klux. I'm just here to return Monique's umbrella.

She places the umbrella next to the counter and turns back for the door.

MC tries once again to apologize. Before he can get a word out Maisy holds up her hand.

                MAISY (CONT.)
    You heard me.

She walks out.

MC sits down across from Dabni.

> MC
> I wish there was something I could do.

Dabni shows her cute smile.

> DABNI
> She likes Fief Te' Loo.

> MC
> Who's he? A chef?

> DABNI
> It's a perfume silly.

> MC
> I thought I smelled something.

Dabni laughs. MC didn't mean to be funny. She looks closer at him for a moment then he directs his attention down to where she's writing.

> DABNI
> What you want to do is take this Avenue right here.

INT. POLICE STATION - DAY

Cletta sits at a sloppy desk in a Brooklyn police station. His face has some dirt marks on it and his shirt is torn. An unshaved, annoyed police officer sits across from him. His tag reads, DE MEECO.

>   DE MEECO
> You're not as lucky as your
> buddies. No mom and dad to come
> down and bail you out.

DeMeeco smirks while jotting down some notes.

Cletta attempts to sound hard.

>   CLETTA
> You can't keep me here.

A man walks by in cuffs with two officers shoving him along. He is at the brink of tears. Cletta's eyes follow every step.

>   CLETTA (CONT.)
> Can you?

DeMeeco appears triumphant.

>   DE MEECO
> We can't. But we'll hold you until
> they get here.

>   CLETTA
> Who are they?

DeMeeco laughs.

EXT. SIDEWALK

MC holds the piece of paper from Dabni. Both of his hands grip the edges as he stands on the sidewalk in front of a building. He looks at the paper, 24442. He looks at the building, 24442. Again at the paper, BIG BROTHER. Again at the building, a sign in the window, BE A BIG BROTHER. Another, EVERYONE NEEDS A COMPANION.

MC walks in. A woman behind the desk greets him. Her tag reads, TANYA.

              TANYA
Hello sir. What can I do for you today?

MC looks around the office and then at Tanya's silk blouse.

              MC
That is a beautiful shirt.

She is taken aback for a moment. She smiles.

              TANYA
Thank you. It's a blouse not a shirt.

              MC
Oh, sorry.

              TANYA
That's fine.

MC looks at one of the posters behind Tanya. It is a small boy, a puppy, and a father figure all running in a field of grass. The boy holds a kite string.

>   MC
> I'm from up north. I used to
> belong to an organization called
> Tag Along.

Tanya smiles.

>   TANYA
> Up in Massachusetts, right?

>   MC
> That's the one.

>   TANYA
> Are you interested in
> participating in Big Brother of
> New York?

>   MC
> That's why I'm here.

Tanya waits for MC to produce his ID.

>   TANYA
> MC, I have to run a background
> check. Some people like to do this
> to meet young boys.

She has a disgusted look.

>   TANYA (CONT.)
> As sickening as that may sound.

                    MC
    I understand. Actually, I don't
    understand. I don't understand why
    they keep sending those kind of
    people to overstuffed jail cells
    when there is so much room at the
    bottom of the ocean.

Without words, her expression shows
agreement.

INT. POLICE STATION - NIGHT

In a dimly lit, cement walled basement
room Cletta sits on a raunchy,
splintered, wooden bench in the same
Brooklyn police station. There are no
bars, just a heavy steel door with an
eight by eight inch window. He stares
at his fingers. His nails are bitten
down as far as they can get.

DeMeeco's face appears in the small
window. He watches for a moment, then
grins. A lock turning brings Cletta to
his feet. DeMeeco enters.

They look at one another.

                DE MEECO
    They're upstairs.

They walk out together.

INT OFFICE

MS. GARRANIET, 50's, grey business suit, hair in a bun, sits at the desk. Her Department of social services I.D. hangs from a chain.

>   MS. GARRANIET
>   Hello young man.

>   CLETTA
>   Hello ma'am.

She smiles and puts out her hand.

>   MS. GARRANIET
>   You can call me Ms. Garraniet. I
>   will be making a file for you down
>   at my office.

>   CLETTA
>   I'm Cletta.

He shakes her hand.

INT. MC'S APARTMENT - LATER

MC sits in his apartment on his computer while watching Ferf dart around the room. The moon is big and bright, shining in the sliding glass door along side his desk.

MC reads a note from another member of what used to be his favorite website.

                    MC
MC, I cannot thank you enough
for the kind words you used to
describe my simple short synopsis
of "A Day in Guadalajara." Yours
were the kindest. I almost threw
my hopes of writing in the trash
can along with my admiration of
this web-site after one overly
critical note and one unnecessary
mauling of my work. Anyway, I just
wanted to say THANKS. Josene.

MC has a proud and sympathetic look.

                 MC (CONT.)
Wow, deep. I'm not alone.

He begins to talk softly to himself
while typing.

                 MC (CONT.)
Josene, your work deserved a
flattering note. It is obvious you
put time and effort into spilling
your feelings on paper as you did.
Even if your trip was not the
main interest of another reader,
someone like myself takes the time
to fall deep into your journey to
become part of it. I did enjoy it.
If I didn't I certainly wouldn't
maul it. It appears that this site
attracts a small percentage of
immature writers who tear apart
works like ours in hopes of making
theirs seem better. Yes, I was

slammed also, and if you have
time, read "Sirens in the Sky"
and let me know if you think I
received a fair assessment. Thanks
MC.

Ferf is finally tuckered out and sprawled on the bed.

>MC (CONT.)
> Good idea little guy, girl,
> whatever.

MC lies next to Ferf, flips on the television and closes his eyes.

Once again the *SWOOSH*, as if a ball is being sucked through a vacuum chute. The *swoosh* is followed by the same Dream child's voice.

>DREAM CHILD
>Second thoughts Grump?

EXT. STREET

DREAM SEQUENCE

Just like the night before, they appear to be walking down the middle of a busy New York street, almost gliding. The restaurant called QUERO GLEANO, other store fronts, moving vehicles, and other pedestrians drift past them. The only sound is their two voices.

                    MC
          I'm not Grump. I left him back in
          Beverly.

                DREAM CHILD
          You sounded just like him at the
          Marigold, Klux.

                    MC
          Have you been speaking to Maisy?

Dream child sounds distant. They still
do not make eye contact.

                DREAM CHILD
          Nope.

                    MC
          Carter? Karu'l? James?

                DREAM CHILD
          Those are some people you should
          be a friend to. Carter can sense
          things boy. Did you realize they
          are black?

                    MC
          I know they're black.

                DREAM CHILD
          It's African American asshole!

MC notices Dabni standing in front of
a nameless coffee shop. He warns Dream
child to be nice.

                    MC
          She is special. Don't say the
          wrong thing.

                    DREAM CHILD
          I got ya lover boy.

                         MC
          I'm serious.

MC walks in front of Dabni. The wind blows by both of them. His voice is echoed.

                    MC (CONT.)
          Dream child. This is a very good
          friend of mine. Without her, you
          and I wouldn't have met.

MC looks down at the top of Dream child's head.

                    MC (CONT.)
          What do we say to a lady?

Dream child smiles. He looks up at MC not making eye contact, then at Dabni.

                    DREAM CHILD
          Get your ass in the kitchen!

MC is shocked. He runs to cover Dream child's mouth and falls flat on his face. He wakes with a start. He rolls over, looks at the television and makes out the picture of a kitchen design show.

INT. FITNESS CENTER - MORNING

Early in the morning, MC walks into the apartment fitness center. He is in wrinkled sweat pants and a sweat shirt that doesn't match. The room is small but well equipped. There are four treadmills, and a number of benches, free weights, and universal exercise machines.

TEE, 20'S, beautiful, walks very fast on a treadmill, her ponytail bouncing in time to her breasts. An overweight man sits on a bench. Sweat drips on the towel around his neck. An overweight woman picks up her empty drink bottle and walks toward the door. MC soaks it all in, holds the door for the woman, then stares at the beauty queen who works up quite a sweat. Her shorts hug her well rounded figure.

MC takes the treadmill on the opposite end less than twenty feet from the beauty. She takes her eyes off of the television in the corner for a short moment to notice MC.

MC glances over at her machine. The overweight man notices and shakes his head with a slight smile.

MC finally gets his machine moving the way he wants. It is obvious that he hasn't been in a gym for quite a while. He looks at the woman.

                    MC
    Good morning.

She looks back, out of breath, with a slight smile.

                    TEE
    Morning.

                    MC
    That is a beautiful blouse.

Tee shakes her head and smiles. She wears a tank top.

                    TEE
    Thanks.

The man shakes his head again as MC stares at the television.

                MC'S VOICE
    There has to be something I can
    strike up a conversation about.
    Please give me an in.

The television news goes to a commercial. It is a cat food ad. A large black and white Balinese leaps across the screen and down to the floor to find his Tristies waiting for him. The glamour beauty sees this and smiles.

MC thinks for a moment, then blurts out.

                    MC
    My cat looks just like him.

She can tell instantly what his agenda is. She joins in the game.

                    TEE
　Oh really, what's his name?

MC not expecting a response fumbles over his tongue.

                    MC
　Far.

He pauses for a second.

                 MC (CONT.)
　Ferf. His name is Ferf.

                    TEE
　Oh that's cute. Did you name him?

She feels her thighs to make MC aware that the treadmill is serving its purpose.

Although Dangie helped with the name, MC takes credit.

                    MC
　I sure did. Thanks.

He is even happier than when he received the smile from Monique.

INT. MORT'S APARTMENT - MORNING

Mort lies in his bed a few minutes before ten AM. The sun tries to shine in a window with thick curtains. Clothes are scattered, his television plays cartoons, his radio plays soft rock. The phone suddenly rings startling him. He picks up his head and looks around, his eyes half open.

> MORT
> What the heck?

He pushes the blankets off revealing his ripped sweat pants, red socks, and tank top. The phone is just in arms reach. He extends himself to pick it up on the eighth ring.

> MORT (CONT.)
> Hello?

INT. MC'S OFFICE

INTERCUT

MC sits at his cubicle. He slashes another day off the calendar. His computer screen shows the normal writers website. He taps a pen against a coffee cup.

> MC
> Sounds like someone had a rough night.

Mort clears his throat.

> MORT
> Hey city boy. What's up in the big apple?

                    MC

What apple?

                   MORT

That's what they call New York.

                    MC

Why? And Who are they?

                   MORT

I don't know.

He rolls over to put his elbows on the bed to hold himself up.

                MORT (CONT.)

How's the love life with all the new babes.

                    MC

Oh man I'm glad you brought it up.

MC's eyes light up.

                 MC (CONT.)

I met the most gorgeous woman on earth this morning at the gym.

Mort holds back a laugh.

                   MORT

What the hell were you doing at a gym?

                    MC

All right. Very funny. I went there because it is included in my new temporary apartment.

He makes a muscle and pokes at it with three fingers.

> MC (CONT.)
> You wouldn't believe this girl.

> MORT
> What happened to Mona, or Monica, whatever her name is?

> MC
> Monique. If it doesn't work out with Tee, I'm still going to try for Monique. But I think Tee likes me.

Mort is slightly sarcastic.

> MORT
> I'm sure she does.

His doorbell buzzes.

> MORT (CONT.)
> I better see who that is.

MC sits, Mr. Gohnz stands over his shoulder.

> MC
> Yea, you get that. I have a lot of business to attend to.

He puts the phone down.

> MC (CONT.)
> Hello Mr. Gohnz. I didn't see you there.

He pretends that he was getting off the phone anyway.

INT. MORT'S APARTMENT

Mort opens his front door. Dangie stands on the opposite side.

INT. MC'S OFFICE

Mr. Gohnz is especially nice.

> MR. GOHNZ
> That is quite all right. Stay on the phone as much as you like.

He pats MC on the back.

> MR. GOHNZ (CONT.)
> How are you enjoying your new apartment?

> MC
> It is spectacular. I wish it was permanent.

> MR. GOHNZ
> That would be nice. But before you go looking for something permanent come see me. I know some people.

> MC
> Thanks sir. That is awfully nice.

MC changes the subject.

> MC (CONT.)

Do you have anything for me to do today?

> MR. GOHNZ

Relax kid. Take some time to learn your way around. Don't worry about work. Explore the internet.

Mr. Gohnz heads back to his office.

> MR. GOHNZ (CONT.)

Take an extended lunch.

He waves his hand over his head. The same attractive young woman hurries over to Mr. Gohnz flapping pages in front of his face again.

MC spins back around, reads Josene's response.

> MC

Hi MC. It seems you always know what to say. Thanks again. I found "Sirens in the Sky" and I read it. And no, it did not receive a fair assessment. There are some things I would change about it, but all in all I really enjoyed it and it was very well written. So what is your age/status? Josene.

He smiles to himself.

> MC (CONT.)
> Wow, another woman to romance. I
> should tell her I'm available, but
> I shouldn't sound desperate.

He stops and rests his head on his fist.

Seconds pass, he raises his head.

> MC (CONT.)
> Or, this is an interesting idea.

He whispers to himself while typing.

> MC (CONT.)
> Hello again Josene. First off,
> thank you for the comments
> regarding "Sirens in the Sky".
> And please, if you think you have
> ideas for it, give it a re-write
> and maybe you can enlighten me. As
> far as my age and status, I came
> up with something interesting.
> Tell me how you feel about this.
> We each write a story. Yours about
> how you picture me. A day in the
> life sort of thing. I'll do the
> same about you. When we're done,
> we'll put them together. Maybe we
> could enter it in the contest. MC.

He sits back with his arms folded, a look of achievement.

He pulls out a scrapbook and writes some notes.

INT. MS. GARRANIET'S OFFICE

Cletta sits at a desk across from Ms. Garraniet. Her office is dimly lit. Two neat stacks of paper sit beside a computer monitor and a phone. Various framed photos of children decorate the book shelf behind her.

She fills out paperwork while he fiddles with a desk ornament, a playground with fake snow circulating as he shakes it. Her glasses sit at the end of her nose as she looks at Cletta.

> MS. GARRANIET
> You're only thirteen and you're attempting to mug undercover subway officers?

Cletta puts the ornament down and looks at her with sorrowful eyes.

> CLETTA
> He looked like a bum.

> MS. GARRANIET
> That doesn't make it any better.

Tanya knocks on the half open door.

> TANYA
> Ms. Garraniet? Is this a bad time?

> MS. GARRANIET
> No. Come right in. He is yours.

She walks over to where Cletta sits nervously.

                TANYA
    Hi, you must be Cletta.

She offers her hand. He hesitates then
shakes it.

                CLETTA
    Hi.

            MS. GARRANIET
    Cletta, Tanya. Tanya, Cletta.

Ms. Garraniet hands some forms to
Tanya.

                TANYA
    We have a big brother waiting for
    you Cletta.

Cletta looks up at Tanya with a half
smile. He seems pleased.

INT. MARIGOLD CAFÉ

Over at the Marigold, Dabni pours a
cup for Maisy who sits at her usual
table. Ned also takes up his usual two
tables with his belongings spread out
behind him.

Dabni and Maisy talk.

                DABNI
    It's not like I have a thing for
    him. There is just something
    appealing about him.

Maisy motions for Dabni to stop pouring.

                    MAISY
  That's enough girl. I got to get
  back to work.

She looks in Dabni's eyes.

                  MAISY (CONT.)
  Once a racist, always a racist my
  daddy taught me.

                  DABNI
  Maybe you should give him a
  chance.

                  MAISY
  Mmmmm Hmmmm. I ain't
  disrespecting my daddy like that.
  The day I give someone like Klux
  a chance is the day I have my own
  umbrella and stop using Monique's.
  Be a love and give this back to
  her.

Maisy holds up the umbrella again.

                  MAISY (CONT.)
  It seems to be clearing up.

                  DABNI
  That's another part of it. He has
  a thing for Monique. He wouldn't
  give me a second look.

MAISY
And Monique wouldn't give him a
second look.

She lifts herself from the seat.

MAISY (CONT.)
I'm just gonna run to the ladies
room.

Dabni wipes the table as Maisy walks
toward the back.

MAISY (CONT.)
Once a Klux, always a Klux.

She reaches the bathroom door.

MC walks in the front door towards
Dabni. Monique walks out of her office
with her eyes glued to a booklet. MC
stares at Monique and becomes distracted
as Dabni turns, they bump into one
another.

DABNI
Oh Klux!

The cup crashes to the floor sending
coffee everywhere.

DABNI (CONT.)
I mean MC, sorry.

MC
Don't you mean klutz?

He bends down to pick up the cup.

Monique looks over angrily at Dabni, then back at her booklet. She pours a cup and turns back toward the office door as Dabni apologizes loud enough for her to hear.

                    DABNI
    My fault sir!

Monique walks back into her office.

                    MC
    That was too nice of you. I should have taken the blame for you. You could get fired.

                    DABNI
    But I know you don't want Monique to think you're a klutz.

                    MC
    How'd you get that impression?

She bends down to wipe the floor.

                    DABNI
    I could just tell.

                    MC
    You still didn't have to do that.

                    DABNI
    No biggie. I've spilled coffee in a few big cities. I still think back home is my favorite place to spill coffee. I suddenly have an urge to call my mom.

MC smiles back.

                    MC
    Speaking of Klutz's and Klux's, I
    was wondering if you could give
    this to Maisy next time she comes
    in.

He hands her a small gift wrapped box with a note.

Her smile grows bigger.

                    DABNI
    Well you're in luck. She's in the
    ladies room.

MC looks to the bathroom door nervous.

                    MC
    I think I'd rather you did it. I
    was just stopping by on my way
    to meet my new little brother and
    thought I'd let you know since you
    sorta set it all up.

                    DABNI
    I understand. Maybe this will make
    her get her own umbrella.

MC doesn't understand.

She takes the box and he rushes out just as Maisy comes from the back.

Ned shakes his head and mumbles to himself.

                    NED
     For God's sake. This is not the
     easiest place to concentrate. Damn
     Marigold Mooch again.

                    MAISY
     What are you smiling about?

Maisy looks at Dabni as she hands her
the gift.

                    DABNI
     Someone came to visit you.

                    MAISY
     What is this?

She begins reading the note.

                 MAISY (CONT.)
     I know there is a phrase for when
     words come out right. I don't know
     if there is one for when words
     come out jumbled. Not giving me
     the time of day has made me more
     than humbled. I'm trying to be a
     writer but no-one ever said I was
     a poet. Please accept this small
     token as a peace offering.

She tears it open and notices it is
signed Klux with the K crossed out.

                 MAISY (CONT.)
     Fief Te' Loo? You had to say
     something.

She appears touched.

> DABNI
> Well? What do you think of him now?

> MAISY
> I'm not that easy. And he didn't even write what the phrase is for when words come out right.

Ned quickly scribbles some notes.

INT. TANYA'S OFFICE

MC walks into the Big Brother office where Cletta now sits in front of the desk facing Tanya. Cletta turns around quickly. He notices MC and quickly remembers him from the subway. He becomes nervous and afraid.

Tanya stands up.

> TANYA
> Right on time MC. I'd like you to meet Cletta, your new little brother.

Sweat breaks out on Cletta's forehead as the two lean in to shake hands. MC looks closely at him puzzled.

> MC
> Hi. Nice to meet you. You look like someone I met before but I can't seem to place it.

Cletta turns his face away.

CLETTA
I just have one of those faces.

Tanya sits down and pulls out a small pamphlet.

TANYA
You just have a couple of forms left to sign MC and then you guys can get acquainted.

MC sits in the chair along side Cletta.

INT. COFFEE SHACK

Over at the coffee shack Kamptin is in his usual spot behind the counter rinsing cups and spoons. Harper and Grump stare at their checkerboard with four black pieces in front of Harper, two of which are kings. Grump has six red pieces, one of which is a king.

The chimes ring and in walk Dangie and Mort arm in arm sharing a laugh.

MORT
Two of your finest brewed Kamptin.

Mort motions for Dangie to take a seat as he pulls out some money.

KAMPTIN
Here you go. You guys a couple now?

Mort lays down three singles on the splintered counter.

                    MORT
          We'll see. Keep the change
          Kamptin.

He walks past Harper and Grump on his way to their usual table.

Harper whispers to Grump whose eyes are half shut.

                    HARPER
          I thought that was Gladstone's
          girl.

He raises his voice towards Mort.

                    HARPER (CONT.)
          Where the hell is Gladstone
          anyway?

                    GRUMP
          What? My turn again?

Mort looks over at them.

                    MORT
          He's still in New York.

                    HARPER
          Since when?

                    MORT
          Since last time we told you.

                    HARPER
          I can't keep up with you kids.

Grump makes an illegal move on the board.

> GRUMP
>
> King me!

Harper places a black checker on one of his own.

> HARPER
>
> Good move old timer.

> GRUMP
>
> I'm red you fool. I never take black!

He turns to Mort.

> GRUMP (CONT.)
>
> Speaking of the blacks, when is Gladstone's funeral?

> MORT
>
> You're a barrel of laughs. You should be back in Vaudeville.

Grump turns back around.

> GRUMP
>
> What does that youngster know about Vaudeville?

Harper stares out the crusty window.

Mort holds onto Dangie's hand and they continue to smile at one another.

EXT. MARIGOLD CAFÉ

The first place MC takes Cletta to is the Marigold Café. MC has his hand on the door ready to pull.

Once again Cletta appears nervous.

                CLETTA
You really think this is a place for children?

                MC
C'mon. This is the first place in the city I made any friends. You'll like it.

                CLETTA
I don't know.

                MC
You like girls?

                CLETTA
Hell yea.

                MC
Well there's one I'd like you to meet.

                CLETTA
Uh oh.

MC opens the door and pushes Cletta softly on the back.

                MC
Let's go.

INT. MARIGOLD CAFÉ

Ned sits in his usual office space.

> NED
> Oh jeez, the Marigold Mooch again. Time to take notes.

Ann walks past Ned and looks to MC and Cletta.

> ANN
> I'm surprised you came back here.

> MC
> What? My little mistaken comment?

> ANN
> Not yours. His.

She points to Cletta and then looks to Monique behind the counter.

> ANN (CONT.)
> Monique, your little friend is here.

Monique looks over.

> MONIQUE
> Oh no.

She steps out from behind the counter and looks at MC.

> MONIQUE (CONT.)
> If you're going to bring your son in here I expect an apology.

MC

I'm sorry, he's not my son.

MC looks down at Cletta.

MC (CONT.)

Why am I apologizing?

MONIQUE

Not you. Him. He said something vulgar to me the other day.

CLETTA

I'm sorry ma'am. That was before my big brother was here.

Monique is satisfied with the apology. She goes back to what she was doing.

MC

Speaking of Big Brother, where is Dabni?

Monique has a look of remembrance.

MONIQUE

Oh yea, that's right. You're the klutz that caused her and I to have words. She needed some time off.

She looks back down.

MC

Fired?

MONIQUE

I could never fire my best.

She pauses and looks at Ann who waits for her to continue.

> MONIQUE (CONT.)
> My second best server.
> She'll be back in a day or two.

Ned watches while jotting down some notes.

MC takes Cletta by the hand and they walk towards the door. They get outside and MC looks down at him.

EXT. MARIGOLD CAFÉ

> MC
> Well, that went well.

> CLETTA
> Yep.

> MC
> What did you say to her?

> CLETTA
> Could you show us your boobs?

> MC
> What did she say?

> CLETTA
> She chased us out.

> MC
> A boy after my own heart.
> And I asked if you like girls. So, who are us?

CLETTA
Oh, just two of my friends and me.
They have parents. That's why they
didn't have to stay at the police
station.

MC
That doesn't sound fair.

CLETTA
Life's not fair.

Cletta looks over at MC while they
continue walking down the city
street.

CLETTA (CONT.)
At least that's what I hear.

MC
At least you won't have to get
your hearing checked. That's right
on the money. So, you want to
visit some friends I made uptown?

CLETTA
Isn't it dangerous uptown?

MC
What do I know? I'm a country boy
from up north. We just have to find
the place. Besides, I have some
free time. My boss has been overly
generous with giving me time away
from the office. Leaving early,
long lunches, no projects. It's a
big difference from what I'm used
to.

                    CLETTA
          Maybe he has a crush on you.

Cletta cracks a smile.

MC slows down. He has a baffled look on his face.

                    MC
          Could that be possible? I've heard
          about that kind of thing.

INT. APARTMENT HALLWAY - LATER

MC and Cletta stand side by side in front of a large steel door labeled 2G.

                    MC
          I know this is the number. I hope
          it's the right building.

MC knocks on the door.

                    CLETTA
          I don't want to walk on those
          streets again. Even though I'm
          a kid from the streets, some of
          those people looked pretty mean.

                    MC
          People look how you make them
          look. If you look at them like
          you're afraid of them, they're
          going to appear mean.

                    KARU'L'S VOICE
          Who's there?

                    MC

It's MC!

The door opens.

                  KARU'L

MC who?

Karu'l looks at them.

              KARU'L (CONT.)
Oh subway man. How you feelin?
Come in.

Karu'l shakes MC's hand and pulls him
inside. Cletta follows.

INT. APARTMENT

              KARU'L (CONT.)
Dad! James! Look who's here!

Carter Bell walks into the living room
with a tremendous smile. James follows.
Cletta takes it all in. He feels a
family warmth as soon as he sees the
three men together.

Carter greets MC with a hug.

                  CARTER
I'm happy we gave you a good
enough feeling for you to return.

He looks behind himself. The newspaper
is spread out on the couch.

CARTER (CONT.)
Have a seat. Boys, move them papers.

He looks to Cletta.

CARTER (CONT.)
Who's this?

MC and Cletta sit next to each other after Karu'l organizes the newspaper.

MC
This is my new little brother. You are the first people I wanted him to meet. Well, besides some girls.

CARTER
I can understand that. So can my boys. Right boys?

Karu'l and James answer at the same time as if it is rehearsed.

KARU'L
Watch how you treat the ladies.

JAMES
Watch how you treat the ladies.

CARTER
That's right.

MC clears Cletta's worry.

MC
That's what I'm teaching my little bro here.

He pats Cletta on the back.

Carter enjoys the response.

                    CARTER
    That's what I wanna hear. Boys. Why
    don't you show.

He holds his hand out to Cletta.

                    CLETTA
    Cletta sir.

                    CARTER
    Why don't you show Cletta your
    room?

Karu'l stands at the refrigerator.

                    KARU'L
    Sure dad. You want a drink first?

Carter looks to MC.

                    CARTER
    MC?

                    MC
    Sure. I'll have the same as last
    time.

                    CARTER
    Two gins.

                    MC
    Do you have any crackers in the
    house?

The boys let out a laugh. Carter gives them a striking look. James quickly loses his smile and brings Cletta into the bedroom.

INT. BEDROOM

Cletta's eyes light up. There is a writing desk, a set of bunk beds, two dressers, and a small table with a television. The room is neatly organized without a spec of dust.

>JAMES
>So, how old are you Cletta?

>CLETTA
>Thirteen. Wow! You have a TV?

He admires the small black and white television with rabbit ears sticking up from it.

>JAMES
>Yea, we're spoiled.

>CLETTA
>I never really watched much TV. I can remember being real young, maybe five or six and there was one in the hospital.

>JAMES
>Why were you in the hospital?

>CLETTA
>I don't know. Just woke up there one day I guess.

                    JAMES
    Well, you can watch our TV
    whenever you like. Say, MC didn't
    mention he had a brother.

Karu'l enters the room.

INT. LIVING ROOM

   MC sits next to Carter.

                    CARTER
    You have to make a boy like Cletta
    into a strong self sufficient young
    man. There are too many wild,
    obnoxious fools running around
    out there due to bad parenting.
    I bring my boys up right. I can't
    tell you how many times the police
    had to visit many of the homes
    of my friends because of their
    children's disrespect for decency.
    And you can tell your friend
    from up north that they were all
    flavors.

MC watches Carter speak with significant
interest.

                    MC
    This is the second time I'm taking
    on this responsibility. I did Tag
    Along back up north for a few
    years.

                    CARTER
    You're a good kid. I'm impressed.
    And I'm not that easy to impress.
    If you ever need any guidance
    during the challenge don't
    hesitate to call.

INT. MC'S APARTMENT - DAWN

At five AM the next morning MC wakes and
hits his alarm clock. He looks into the
living room where Cletta snores on the
couch. MC shakes him lightly.

                    MC
    I'm off to the fitness center.
    You're welcome to tag along.

Cletta mumbles in his sleep.

                    CLETTA
    What floor is it on? I'll meet you
    there.

                    MC
    The second.

MC quietly leaves.

INT. FITNESS CENTER

MC walks in. He is in a different pair of
wrinkled sweat pants and another sweat
shirt that doesn't match. Everything is
like a repeat of his first trip.

Tee, the same beautiful and sexy woman walks extra fast on the same treadmill as before. Her blonde pony tail bounces with each step. This time she greets MC when he enters.

                    TEE
          Good morning.

                    MC
          Hi Tee. Are you still on that
          thing?

They share a laugh.

The overweight man sits on the bench with a towel around his neck. He shakes his head at the joke. One difference from earlier is another attractive young girl on a stationary bike off to the side. Tee looks over at her.

                    TEE
          This is my neighbors little girl,
          Amanda, we call her MANDY.

Mandy waves to MC.

                    MC
          Nice to meet you Mandy.

He notices that she is pretty but something about her seems young. She is one of those thirteen year old girls who appear to be over seventeen.

MC takes the same treadmill as last time. Just as he gets on, Cletta bangs his arm against the door.

> CLETTA
> Ouch!

MC climbs off the treadmill to let him in. He opens the door.

> MC
> You need to swipe a card for the door to open or else you can hurt yourself.

Cletta smirks.

> CLETTA
> Really?

They both laugh. Cletta stares at Tee for a moment, then at Mandy who stares back. Cletta's eyes then quickly go back to Tee. He whispers.

> CLETTA (CONT.)
> Oh man.

MC makes the introductions.

On the television the same Tristies commercial plays. Tee smiles.

> TEE
> Look, it's Ferf!

MC smiles then looks to Cletta.

                    CLETTA
          Ferf doesn't look.

MC cuts him off.

                    MC
          Cletta, why don't you tell the
          girls how you like Big Brother so
          far?

Cletta is obviously cheerful.

                    CLETTA
          There's no one like MC. I wish he
          came here seven years sooner.

INT. MORT'S APARTMENT - LATER

Dangie kneels on Mort's bed in dark blue jeans, a tee shirt, and socks. Mort sits at his desk across from her, his eyes glued to her. Bright sun light glares on the television screen. The room is cleaner than normal.

He slowly makes his way over to her. He appears giddy, a bit awkward and goofy.

                    MORT
          Do you like this show?

He leans over to grab the remote. Dangie places her hand on his chest and their lips meet.

The kiss lasts for close to four seconds when the phone rings startling them both.

> MORT (CONT.)
> Yea?

INT. MC'S OFFICE

INTERCUT

> MC
> Hey Mort. Whatcha doin?

MC sits at his cubicle. His normal website is up on his computer.

> MORT
> Oh, uh, hi MC.

Mort looks to Dangie shrugging his shoulders.

> MORT (CONT.)
> Something important?

> MC
> Nah, just thought I'd say hello.

> MORT
> Well um.

> MC
> Look, I wanted to apologize to you and Dangie.

> MORT
> It's okay.

Mort looks lost.

> MC
>
> Do you know why?

> MORT
>
> I guess not.

> MC
>
> I'm sorry. I totally forgot to give you and Dangie a goodbye gift. You know I never like to leave without giving something.

> MORT
>
> It's okay. It's okay.

> MC
>
> Really?

Dangie begins kissing Mort's neck. He becomes fluttered.

> MORT
>
> Yea, yea.

> MC
>
> Is this a bad time buddy?

Mort leans over for another kiss.

> DANGIE
>
> Is he still there? What he say?

Mort drops the phone. He whispers in Dangie's ear.

> MORT
>
> Sorry no goodbye gift.

                    DANGIE
What?

                    MORT
No goodbye gift. MC didn't give us any.

                    DANGIE
Oh. He gave me one.

                    MORT
Really?

                    DANGIE
Yea.

                    MORT
What?

                    DANGIE
I'm kissing it.

                    MORT
I guess he gave me one too.

They continue to kiss. They knock the photo of Mort, MC, and Dangie to the floor. It drops next to the phone.

                    MC'S VOICE
Mort? Mort? Are you messing with me?

The two of them lay back on the bed.

MC looks at the receiver and smirks.

                    MC
I hope everything is okay over
there.

He goes back to the computer screen to
read Josene's note.

                    MC
Hi MC. I went ahead and began my
own version of "Sirens in the Sky"
like you suggested. I renamed it
"Blaring Siren" and I turned your
main character Timmy into a fire
fighter. I hope you don't mind. I
also loved your idea of a day in
the life and began writing that as
well. Let me know your feelings.
Your friend, Josene.

MC does not hesitate a response.

                 MC (CONT.)
Josene. The fire fighter idea
sounds inspiring. Any reason in
particular you went with it? I
started putting notes together
on the day in the life also. Now
that I know you like it, I will
continue. Talk to you soon. MC.

He clicks the send button and turns
around to see Mr. Gohnz standing behind
him.

                  MR. GOHNZ
You're doing a marvelous job son.

                    MC
    Hello Mr. Gohnz. Do you have
    anything for me to do?

Mr. Gohnz smiles and rubs his chin.

                 MR. GOHNZ
    Why don't you head out a little
    early and entertain that new
    little brother of yours?

He begins to walk off.

MC is pleased as well as confused.

                    MC
    Marvelous job? I haven't done
    anything since I started here.

He continues whispering.

                 MC (CONT.)
    A little early? I've only been here
    a few hours.

He begins shutting down his computer and slashes another day off the calendar.

Mr. Gohnz is not too far off in the distance when the same lovely woman, MISS BEOWD, confronts him with paperwork. She begins waving it once again and then speaks softly. She sounds upset.

                 MISS BEOWD
    How much longer are you going to
    let this kid go on living away
    from home to adapt in a place
    where he has no future?

He pulls her gently to the side and puts his index finger to his lips.

>   MR. GOHNZ
> Shhhhh. Quiet Miss Beowd. I'm
> still not sure how I'm going to
> break it to him.

>   MISS BEOWD
> Well you better do it soon. His
> paychecks will be ending before
> long.

She walks off in a bit of a huff.

MC turns from his computer and watches her walk off. Mr. Gohnz waves gently.

MC looks at him sadly until Mr. Gohnz turns around. MC whispers under his breath.

>   MC
> Maybe he does have a crush on me.
> That's sick.

MONTAGE

Harper and Grump play checkers at the coffee shack.

Mort and Dangie walk in holding hands and laughing. Kamptin smiles at them.

MC and Cletta at Carter Bell's apartment. Karu'l and James walk Cletta into their room. The three of them get comfortable on the floor in front of the small television. Carter sits next to MC, hands him a glass of gin. They tap their glasses together.

MC writes in his scrapbook in his dark apartment. Ferf lies next to him.

Dabni stands next to Maisy sitting at a table at the Marigold Café. Maisy shakes her head in disagreement to what Dabni tries to explain. Monique looks on from her office. She appears angry. Ned looks on and jots notes, speaks into a cell phone and types on his laptop.

MC writes in his scrapbook in his dark apartment. Ferf lies next to him.

MC and Cletta at the gym. They talk and laugh with Tee and Mandy. The overweight man looks on. The Tristies commercial comes on the television. Tee points to it.

MC, Cletta, Tee, and Mandy sit at an outdoor table at QUERO GLEANO having lunch. MC opens his wallet. The picture of Dangie stares back at him. He looks sad for a moment.

Mort and Dangie pull in front of Mort's apartment in the Angel of Lost Parts. She leans over for a kiss.

MC continues to make slash marks on his calendar. The last day of the complimentary apartment approaches quickly.

INT. MC'S OFFICE - DAY

Mr. Gohnz stands with a tear in his eye behind MC who types away on his favorite website. MC notices him.

>							MC
>Good morning Mr. Gohnz. I am ready to discuss what you offered a couple of weeks ago.

Mr. Gohnz composes himself.

>							MR. GOHNZ
>What is that son?

>							MC
>Are you okay?

>							MR. GOHNZ
>I'll be fine. What is it you wanted to discuss?

>							MC
>Remember you said before I go looking for somewhere permanent to live I should come see you because you know some people? Here I am to see you sir.

MC appears very happy.

Mr. Gohnz rubs his temple and grunts.

MR. GOHNZ
You're not going to make this any
easier are you?

He looks over his shoulder and sees Miss
Beowd glancing in their direction.

MC's happiness turns to worry.

MR. GOHNZ (CONT.)
Look son.

He sits on MC's desk.

MR. GOHNZ (CONT.)
There was a mistake.

MC
I don't understand. I couldn't
have made a mistake.

MR. GOHNZ
Not you. Us. You see, the company,
actually Miss Beowd, miscalculated
the needs during this whole
relocation project.

He looks over at Miss Beowd once again.
She walks off.

MC
So my services are no longer
needed.

MR. GOHNZ
Unfortunately.

MC
I understand sir. Actually I'm not
surprised.

MR. GOHNZ
That is very big of you MC.

MC
Now I see why you were so nice to me.

Mr. Gohnz clears his throat.

MR. GOHNZ
Yes son. Let me know if you need any help gathering your things.

MC shuts down his computer and throws some items in his Trenis' Times bag.

MC
I'm good. I know it's not your fault and you've been great about everything. I'm just sorry I don't have a going away gift for you.

MC takes a few steps toward the elevators.

Mr. Gohnz' voice cracks.

MR. GOHNZ
Just spending the little time we had together was a gift to me.

MC turns around, he looks uncomfortable. He mumbles under his breath.

MC
He can't have a crush on me.

He looks at Mr. Gohnz who gives a wink. MC rushes into an elevator.

INT. CARTER'S APARTMENT - LATER

MC stands at Carter's door as it opens.

CARTER
Why the long face boy?

He motions for MC to have a seat while he walks into the kitchen.

MC
Looks like plans have changed.

Carter pours two gins.

CARTER
You can't stay here in New York no longer, right?

MC
How'd you know?

CARTER
I can sense things boy.

MC
That's spooky.

Carter puts a glass in front of MC and takes a seat.

CARTER
I know you say things as innocent as can be but some folks take offense to things like spook or even cracker like you said the other day. It's not your fault. The world has been creating words for

one person to insult another since the beginning of time. Before long, words like bunny rabbit or preciousness will have the same affect as saying dammit after God or mother after your. The world is a strange place. A gift gone spoiled.

MC
At least I'll be taking home some of your wisdom Carter. I wish I had something to give to you and the boys.

CARTER
Boy, you done give us enough. That is as long as you ain't taking Cletta with you.

MC
Oh no sir. I haven't even thought about that.

CARTER
He's inside with the boy's right now. They the best of friends since you came around. Karu'l even got the boy work. Look, I love the boy like he's my own. Your short impression on him was magical. If you promise to take on a new Tag Along back up north, Cletta will be our new little brother.

MC
You got a deal there Carter.

                    CARTER
You going to that coffee place
you been talking about before you
leave?

                    MC
I haven't given that much thought
either. I guess I have to say
goodbye to them over there.

He looks upward.

                MC (CONT.)
I can't forget about Dabni.

                    CARTER
As much as I am against that over
priced yuppie mud-water, me and
the boys will come by to say so
long.

MC has an unforgettable smile.

                    MC
That would be a memory to take
back home.

Carter puts his sock covered feet up
on the coffee table, grins and takes a
sip of his gin.

INT. MC'S APARTMENT - MORNING

MC wakes up early the next morning.
All of his belongings are packed beside
his apartment door. He grabs the pet
carrier that holds Ferf.

                    MC
        C'mon you genderless prize. We got
        work to do.

    They exit the apartment.

INT. FITNESS CENTER

    MC enters the exercise room. Tee and
    Mandy finish up their workout.

    MC is uncomfortable.

                    MC
        Tee. Hi. I want to say something
        to you.

    She approaches him and holds his arm.

                    TEE
        Is everything okay?

                    MC
        Yes and no. I have to head back
        home. Up north.

                    TEE
        Oh, that's too bad.

                    MC
        I wanted to give you a gift. I
        don't like saying goodbye without
        giving something.

    He holds the pet carrier out and opens
    the door.

    Tee almost melts.

                    TEE
          Awwww. Is this little Ferf?

She holds Ferf and looks closely at
its face.

                    TEE
          You said Ferf looked like the cat
          on TV.

MC becomes shy.

                    MC
          I have an apology.

He looks down.

                    MC (CONT.)
          I couldn't have started a
          conversation by saying, that cat
          doesn't look like my cat, could I?

                    TEE
          I guess not. Why aren't you taking
          Ferf back home with you?

                    MC
          I sorta promised him no more car
          trips. It's not nice to break a
          promise to your cat.

Tee holds Ferf up higher.

MC regains courage.

                    MC (CONT.)
          So, maybe we could get together
          for a date or something if you're

ever in my town or I'm ever back
in your town?

She has an apologetic smile.

> TEE
> MC. I like you. I like you a lot.
> But as a friend. We can stay
> friends.

He is crushed.

> MC
> Sure. I was just saying. You know?

She continues to hold Ferf up while looking underneath, she changes the subject.

> TEE
> Is Ferf a boy or a girl?

He laughs slightly.

> MC
> Good question. I'm not sure. My
> girlfriend picked it out.

> TEE
> Mandy, you have to say goodbye to
> MC.

Mandy walks over to shake his hand.

> MC
> Can you guys share Ferf? I didn't
> bring you anything Mandy.

                    MANDY
Don't worry. You gave me a better
gift.

                    MC
What was that?

                    TEE
I think she has a thing for
Cletta.

Mandy smiles.

INT. MC'S APARTMENT - MOMENTS LATER

MC returns to his apartment for one
last look around.

                    MC
What the hell. One last call, it's
on the company.

He walks over and dials.

INT. MORT'S APARTMENT

INTERCUT

Back in Beverly Mort sits alone in his
apartment at his desk. Cartoons are on
the television and music plays softly
as the phone rings. The photo of Mort,
MC, and Dangie is back on the night
stand where the phone sits.

He picks up the phone.

MORT
Hey! I was just thinking of you.
How goes it in the big city?

MC
It's not easy. I can remember
when everything was simpler. You,
me, Dangie, the people on Ludlum
Avenue and Carter Bend. Now it's
all work, chasing dreams, and
mixing positives.

Mort looks at the photo next to the
phone. He picks it up and holds it while
staring at each young face slowly.

MORT
I guess our moms were right. We do
grow up right before their eyes.

MC pulls the phone away for a moment
and looks at it.

MC
Mort? Is that really you?

MORT
What's wrong?

MC
That sounded too deep to be the
Mort I know.

MORT
I'm too deep? What the hell is
mixing positives?

                    MC
I don't know. There's a phrase for
what I really want to say. Like
when meeting some girl in a gym,
in a coffee shop, on a writer's
website. Quick blurbs about your
days, simple greetings, there's a
word for that. Or two words for
that.

                   MORT
You're the writer.

                    MC
Not according to some people.

                   MORT
Still down about those sour
comments buddy? I got some news
that'll cheer you right up.

                    MC
Really? Cause the reason I called
was to give you some big news.

                   MORT
You sound like you need to go
first.

                    MC
I'm coming back home!

Mort is shocked. After a moment he
speaks.

                    MORT
    Well, if you're coming home, my
    big news can wait till you get
    here.

EXT. NEW YORK CITY STREET - MOMENTS LATER

MC approaches his car that he hasn't so much as peeked at during his stay in New York City. He opens the car door, the smell smacks him in the face. A bottle or two, crumpled paper bags, and a corroded head of lettuce fall to the street next to his feet.

Snoring comes from the back seat, a closer look reveals the homeless man he met weeks earlier. MC shakes and startles him.

                HOMELESS MAN
    Pom a dollar. Pom a quarter. Bar
    since. Car a home.

MC smirks.

                    MC
    At least now I know what that last
    part means.

INT. MARIGOLD CAFÉ - LATER

At the café, Ann runs around picking up after customers trying to make it through another morning rush. Dabni is not there and Monique only sticks her head out to check once in a while.

The crowd gets smaller and smaller to reveal Ned taking up his usual space. He types away at his laptop.

In walk Carter, Cletta, Karu'l, and James. Cletta knows his way around. He scans the area for Monique.

Ned pops his head up for a second, sips his latte, makes a displeased face towards Carter and the family, and resumes his business.

            CARTER
Shall we take a seat?

Carter looks to Cletta.

MC's car pulls up outside the window.

EXT. MARIGOLD CAFÉ

He is snagged by his umbrella getting out. He tries to squeeze it back in with the piles of luggage, it's a no go. He puts the umbrella under his arm with the Trenis' Times bag and walks with it.

MC enters.

INT. MARIGOLD CAFÉ

The group lets out an unrehearsed holler.

                    THE GROUP
    Surprise!

Ned looks up again.

                    NED
    Oh Lord. The Marigold Mooch is
    still in town.

He lowers his head and tries to block
out the commotion.

Ann peers over and smiles. She gives a
quick wave. MC reciprocates. She heads
toward the coffee pots.

Monique's head pops out to see what the
festivities are about. She whispers.

                    MONIQUE
    Pssst. Ann. Is that the guy that
    always bothers Dabni?

                    ANN
    I don't think she would call it a
    bother.

                    MONIQUE
    What does he want?

                    ANN
    I think he's just celebrating
    something with his friends.

Cletta and MC notice Monique at the
same time. They both give her a child
like grin and wave.

Monique grits her teeth, waves back and continues her conversation with Ann.

>   MONIQUE
> I thought he didn't like black
> people.

>   ANN
> I swear. No one can give the poor
> guy a chance.

Ann brings a regular coffee over to MC.

>   ANN (CONT.)
> Here you go hun. Anything for your
> friends?

>   CLETTA
> I'll take these cookies. And I'd
> like to pay twice if that's all
> right?

Cletta takes the gourmet cookies off the shelf and holds up a ten dollar bill.

>   ANN
> That would be fine. Just a bit
> strange.

Ann takes the ten and MC follows her to the register.

>   MC
> Can I ask you something Ann?

>   ANN
> She quit.

MC

How'd you know what I was going to ask?

ANN

Call me a psychic. It wasn't that hard to tell. I know your eyes were on Monique, but I could tell your heart was wrapped up in Dabni.

MC

Wow.

ANN

Yea, I'm good. So what brings the gang here?

MC

I'm heading back home. They're giving me the royal send off.

ANN

Couldn't handle the city life?

MC

The city couldn't handle me.

He cracks a smile.

ANN

I can see why she was so crazy about you.

MC

Well, there's always Dangie to settle for back home.

                    ANN
No one should ever just settle.

                    MC
Thanks again for everything Ann.

                    ANN
You too. And good luck kid.

She extends her hand and they shake.

MC returns to the table. First he approaches Cletta. They hug.

                    MC
I guess this is it little brother.

                  CLETTA
Thanks for all the new friends big brother. I could never have got on the straight and narrow path without you.

Cletta slips the cash that was stolen on the subway into MC's Trenis' Times bag.

MC moves on down the line as Maisy's face can be seen through the window in front of MC's car.

MC holds onto Karu'l's arm with his right hand and James' with his left. Karu'l wipes his eye.

                  KARU'L
Thanks for the new brother and the fun.

                    JAMES
    You're a good man MC. Just stay off
    them subway's.

James causes them to laugh.

Carter grabs onto MC especially firm.

                    CARTER
    You're a special boy. Anything,
    anytime. The Bell family is always
    here for ya.

Maisy has to rub her eyes while entering
the Marigold.

                    MAISY
    I can't hardly believe this. You
    all friends with Kl- I mean Lux
    here?

                    KARU'L
    He's one of the good ones ma'am.

Karu'l smiles to Maisy.

She scratches her head.

                    MAISY
    Maybe Dabni was right.

She holds onto MC.

                    MAISY (CONT.)
    I'm sorry Lux. She is the one for
    you.

MC hands her his umbrella.

                    MC
> It looks cloudy Maisy. You might
> need this.

He heads out to his car as they all stand at the window waving goodbye. Ned looks on in disgust.

EXT. CARTER BEND - DAY

Just like a few weeks earlier, a soft breeze brings slight movement to the orange leaves that barely cling to the maples up and down Carter Bend. The bronze statue of Vince Carter still sits proudly guarding the cul-de-sac at the end of the road.

The barber shop, gas station, ice cream shop, grocery store, library, and the coffee shack come into view. Friendly faces pass on the street.

INT. COFFEE SHACK

Harper and Grump sit at their regular table. Something is different. The checkerboard is gone. It has been replaced with a candyland board. Still neither of them pays any attention to the game.

Grump shakes his head and blinks his eyes rapidly. He looks around the room noticing the chimes ring as Mort and Dangie enter.

                    HARPER
    Mornin Dangie.

Harper lifts his head for a moment and
then looks back down at the candyland
board shrugging his shoulders.

                HARPER (CONT.)
    Am I red or black?

Grump stares out the window.

Mort and Dangie stand speaking to
Kamptin. They laugh.

Grump smiles. Harper leans over to
look out the window with him. He also
becomes excited.

The chimes ring again and Harper
smiles.

                HARPER (CONT.)
    Hey Gladstone, would you mind?

He holds his coffee cup up. Grump
follows suit.

                      MC
    Sure thing Harper, Grump.

MC puts his bags down as Mort and
Dangie make their way over to greet
him. They exchange hugs.

Once they settle down Kamptin places
three cups of coffee and a package of
crackers on the counter.

                    KAMPTIN
          These are on the house.

                      MC
          Thanks Kamptin. How've you been?

Kamptin gives a big smile and a thumbs
up to MC.

MC, followed by Mort and Dangie, brings
the coffees to Harper and Grump. He
places them down on their table.

                    MC (CONT.)
          Hey candyland. Can I play the
          winner?

Mort laughs.

                    MORT
          There are no winners at this
          table.

Dangie slaps Mort and they hug gently.
MC becomes confused.

Mort looks at MC while in the middle
of the hug.

                    MORT (CONT.)
          I told you I had big news. We're
          getting married. You're my best
          man!

MC's coffee cup falls to the floor and
spills. He stares at the two of them.

MORT (CONT.)
Look. He's all choked up. I told you he'd be speechless.

DANGIE
I hope he's not this speechless when he makes the toast at the wedding.

Dangie looks concerned.

The chimes ring once again and MC stares at the door. His eyes follow a customer who enters.

MORT
He's really in shock.

DANGIE
MC are you okay?

Still not a word from MC.

MORT
Stop messing around. What's wrong?

DANGIE
Mort do something!

MC continues to stare at the counter. His mouth and eyes go from lost to confusion to contempt to extreme happiness.

A voice calls over.

VOICE
Need help cleaning that spill?

Dabni stands in front of the counter holding two coffee cups.

                    MC
    Wh- wh- what are you doing here?

He takes a step toward her. She puts her cups down on the counter.

                    DABNI
    I was taking a trip up to Maine
    with my dad. We just stopped for a
    cup.

                    MC
    I thought I'd never see you again.

                    DABNI
    I'm glad we chose this exit for
    gas.

                    MC
    That's the nicest thing anyone's
    ever said to me.

MC goes in for a hug.

                    DABNI
    We can't lose touch ever again.

Dabni squeezes him tight.

The chimes ring once again.

Mort and Dangie look at each other with some confusion. A small African American child stands next to Mort. It is Dream child.

Mort continues to stare at MC and Dabni.

> MORT
> Who is she and what is she doing here?

Dangie shrugs. Dream child looks at Mort.

> DREAM CHILD
> Hell if I know. I told her to get her ass in the kitchen.

> DANGIE
> You must be MC's new Tag Along.

Dangie puts out her hand. Dream child shakes it.

> DANGIE (CONT.)
> He sure has his hands full once again.

> DREAM CHILD
> The name's Gladstone. I play football. One day I'll be on the New York Jets! Nice to meet you white folks.

Dream child moves over and sits on Grumps lap.

> DREAM CHILD
> Candyland! Can I play?

Grump doesn't know if he should push him off or hold him tight. Something makes him hold on tight.

Mort whispers to Dangie.

> MORT
> That's the long lost grandson I told you about.

Dangie has a look of shock.

MC has never looked as happy as he does at this moment. He holds on tight to Dabni, he notices Dream child. He is confused how his dream came to reality but he happily accepts it.

> MC
> I got my girl. I got my new little brother. Now all I need is a job.

A sound that has never been heard before in the coffee shack is heard. Everyone's attention is on the bags by the door. A closer look reveals his Boston Herald phone ringing.

INT. MARIGOLD CAFÉ - NIGHT

It is dark, cold and lonely. The only one seen on the premises is Ned. He reads a review of his most recent story. It is the one he concocted of the notes he took whenever MC showed up at The Marigold. He slurps on a latte.

> NED
> I am exceedingly depleted. The ramblings from page one to page twenty-one exasperated my every

> ounce of energy. Sound familiar? Your story about my experience is not going to make it. Reason being, you are missing all of the golden words offered by one Carter Bell. If you would have considered that, you may have had a best seller instead of living in a best cellar. You should also consider using the two words for meeting some girl in a gym, in a coffee shop, on a writer's website. Quick blurbs about your days, simple greetings.
> It's all work, chasing dreams, and exchanging pleasantries. The wealthiest of writers have no fortunes in money, although they live to share all they create. Yours Truly, The Marigold Mooch.

Anger fills Ned's face.

>   NED (CONT.)
> You no good son of a bitch!

He continues reading another portion of the website.

>   NED (CONT.)
> Third prize goes to Sirens in the sky.

He scrolls down.

                    NED (CONT.)
          Second prize goes to Blaring
          Siren.

     He continues to scroll.

                    NED (CONT.)
          First prize goes to A Day in the
          Life?

     He is put out.

                    NED (CONT.)
          What? Where is my prize? My story
          was the best! This site is fixed!

     He begins to choke on his latte.

     Monique walks out of her office.

                    MONIQUE
          Oh, you're still here?

     Ned tries to regain his composure.

                    NED
          Are you happy to see me? Or are
          you just exchanging pleasantries?

EXT. CARTER BEND - DAY

  MC and Dabni stand in front of the
  Vince Carter statue holding hands.

Dedicated to Vince Carter.
A brave soul who built a place
for all of us to escape the wrath
of hatred and prejudice. May love
and freedom always reign in Beverly MA.
Or maybe a passerby can just remember
why this town was created.

FADE OUT.

THE END.

About the author

ferf ziamond is a pen name representing a colorless, ageless, genderless tale teller who introduces a different concept. Movie style writing with screenplay edition included.

Printed in Great Britain
by Amazon